STOLEN

by Kate Valery

To my dear former boss and friendly co-worker Mr. Ray Musgrave from author.
Kate Valery

RoseDog 🐾 Books

PITTSBURGH, PENNSYLVANIA 15222

ISBN: 978-0-8059-8918-2
Library of Congress Control Number: 2006933394

Printed in the United States of America

First Printing

For more information or to order additional books,
please contact:
RoseDog Books
701 Smithfield Street
Third Floor
Pittsburgh, Pennsylvania 15222
U.S.A.
1-800-834-1803
www.rosedogbookstore.com

Dedication:

To my dear girls
Martina and Isabella

Stolen offers us a plot that is extreme and unique. Kate Valery does a good job in revealing the internal workings of the characters. Overall *Stolen* is a fascinating tale. This love triangle story is full of outrageous jealousy, deceit, suicide, passion, and guilt. Some sex scenes are hot and intense. Having been a victim of theft, will Nick become a stolen treasure himself? —Inna Spice, Author of *Erotica*

Stolen is an impressive and even shocking book. It is full of opposites: death and incarnation, honesty and deceit, devotion and betrayal, defaming and purity. The characters defy the reader's expectation and lead you to surprising places. The most touching to me is the fact paintings are one of the leading characters of the book. —Victor Vanslov, Academician, Member of the Board of Russian Academy of Art

ACKNOWLEDGMENT

I wish to thank my kind and subtle intellectual psychologist Dr. Joe Daniluk for his priceless help and advice, and my dear friend for many years Cindie Thompson, who always was close and gave me a hand when I need it.

In the production of the book itself, I thank all those who helped with the manuscript, and particularly:

For editing – my dear American sister Erin Bouma, the ESL teacher, author of 7 workbooks;

For finding some striking words for this book – Ms. Jean Schultz, my very nice former boss in business;

For security and police consulting – Mr. Larry Ellis, the perfect specialist, security coordinator of the United Nations.

Especially I want to thank my husband Valery, who carried me through life, taught me what the true love is, and tolerated all the burdens of being the writer's husband.

All of the above great people gave a chance to my book *STOLEN* to appear in this world.

Enjoy your reading, my dear ones!

Chapter 1

"ALANA, ALANA!" THE WALKIE-TALKIE excitedly called her name. "Come here! As fast as you can! There's a crazy patient here!"

This call came so suddenly, that Alana Miller, a pretty twenty-two-year-old, quivered. She was sitting in an armchair in the conference hall, relaxing and watching a National Geographic channel program about travel around Germany. Alana had only turned on the television because she was bored and had wanted to check the weather forecast, but the show about Berlin had caught her eye.

The host talked about St. Peter's Cathedral, which was fully restored after the Second World War, one half of it in a blue glass.

The sun shone through the glass and created the miraculous effect of another world. It was so amazing, so uplifting, with a spirit of holiness! The show and the drawn-out peal of the large bell added to this powerful sensation. It was beautiful enough to carry one away to paradise.

Alana's eyes were glued to the screen. Her interest in Germany, due to her German roots, led her to dream of one day visiting there. Her pregnant German mother had immigrated to the U.S. as a political refugee, delivering her child in Minneapolis as a new American citizen.

"Alana!" the panicked voice on the radio called out. "Room 105! And hurry!"

The voice was that of her partner Jim. He was a very big and strong young man and she was startled to hear the hysteria in his voice. Was there something going on that he couldn't handle? Usually the 'crazy patients' were merely eighty-year-old women suffering from Alzheimer's who wanted to climb out of bed and waltz off to a shopping center to have their hair done. It wouldn't be hard for Jim to restrain them.

"Ten-four", Alana barked in acknowledgement. Then, irritated by the radio interruption, she turned off the TV and quickly locked the empty conference hall. She raced down the back fire-escape stairs since Jim must be in the Emergency Department on the main floor.

1

"Cell B!" she faintly heard Jim yell over the radio. "Faster, Alana! He's dying!"

Why can't Jim call the doctors or nurses if someone is dying? Alana thought, her annoyance growing. How can I possibly help? Declare Code Blue, or something?

When she burst into Cell B, a big fight was underway. A young male patient was trying to free himself from his bed straps, thrashing around, but Jim and two nurses had pinned his arms. Bloody sheets and a blanket testified to the struggle, as did the red-spattered staff uniforms. The patient's hands were blood-soaked and the IV beside him had been torn out of his arm.

"Help us! Quickly! Hold him down," one of the nurses shouted to Alana, "and I'll give him a shot."

Alana tried to take over from the nurse and restrain the patient's arm but it wasn't easy. The man continued to jerk and wiggle, trying to escape. For a split second his knotted fist came close to her eyes and she saw in horror that his entire wrist bandage was drenched in red liquid which was dripping down his arm toward the crook of his elbow.

His face was hidden from her because he was turned the other way. She could only see the blonde matted hair on the back of his head and hear his crazed growls. Alana felt both scared and uneasy, but she managed to hold his arm as tightly as possible.

The nurse with a needle in her hand re-appeared at the bedside and, without hesitating, gave the man's upper thigh the shot. The belts on the hospital bed had held his legs fast through the entire melee.

"Leave me alone!" the man screamed. "I hate you all! I won't live! I can't anymore!"

He began crying and sobbing, but it was already obvious that the medication was taking affect. Very soon the epicenter of the storm began to calm down. His exhausted, damp arms dropped on the bed and his weary head relaxed on the pillow as his eyes began closing. At last he was sleeping, though his wracked body was still convulsing occasionally due to the build up of muscle tension.

"What the hell," Jim grumbled, examining his own disheveled figure. His uniform sleeve and front was spotted in red, his shirt pulled out of the belted slacks. "He's made a mess of everything! What a crazy guy!"

"I got smeared, too," Alana said, still breathing heavily after the violent encounter. She looked down in dismay at her once-white shirt with the black-and-gold logo of the security company. "I need to change. Luckily I have an extra shirt in my locker." She moved toward the door.

2

"Anybody know what in the hell happened to this guy? An accident? I've never seen so much blood around here."

"You can go now. We'll re-bandage him," one of the nurses told her. The other nurse was already busy changing the patient's bed sheets.

Alana and Jim stepped out into the hallway.

"It's terrible," Alana murmured, still trembling. "I've never seen anything quite like it in my life. It was so sudden. I was in the quiet conference hall when…"

Jim made a wry face at his partner.

"He put up such a fight before you came. You can't imagine," he said. "Bloody monster! He attempted suicide. I don't know…Someone found him and called an ambulance. He had lost a lot of blood, but as soon as they patched him up he turned aggressive. Did you hear his scream that he doesn't want to live? I just don't get it. Life is so amazing! How could anyone want to end it all?"

"You couldn't possibly know what made him to do it, Jim," Alana replied, shrugging her shoulders. "Maybe he just lost his love or something like that."

"C'mon, Alana. He's handsome enough to find a new girl. Big deal! Even for me with my low salary, it's not a problem. But for him – he's a millionaire! Well, I always believed they were crazy and now I've seen one for myself. Those rich guys choke on all their money and don't even value the good life they've got. How stupid can you be?"

"How do you know all that, Jim? That he is a millionaire?"

"I was on front desk and I asked the paramedics who brought him in where they found him. They said at Twins South. I'm sure you know what that means."

Alana nodded. The entire city knew that Twins South was the privileged district of Minneapolis – right in the parkland of the river valley. Every house there was a real palace, each uniquely designed by world-famous architects. Ordinary people drove through the area only on excursions, since they weren't exactly welcome in the neighborhood.

Jim continued, laughing, "The paramedics even told me that they were lost inside his mansion and had trouble finding the front door. That man lives in the paradise and he thinks it's hell. He doesn't even want it. You know, they are really spoiled, all those millionaires. Their life is so good…"

Alana was listening with one ear as they walked to the locker room. She had never heard Jim go on about rich people before, but she'd heard some of his other surface prejudices from time to time.

"In fact, their life is so good that their next step might take them to heaven," Jim went on. "This guy seems in a really big hurry to get there on his own. You know, Alana, if somebody would give me their money, I could figure out what to do with it all right. I'd have no problem, making my life absolutely beautiful. Come to think of it, it's already beautiful. I just hope this bloody idiot doesn't have AIDS or something, since we all got a fair amount of his blood on us!"

"I hope so, too," Alana sighed. She shook her head in dismay as she waved goodbye and disappeared behind the locker room door.

She went to the restroom and intensively washed her hands and face not once, but twice. Then she changed her uniform, glancing into the mirror, satisfied with her appearance.

Alana didn't use any makeup; she didn't really need to as she had a fresh, youthful face. Her large gray eyes and long dark eyelashes were framed by her beautiful, wavy nut-brown hair. She usually wore her hair down, but security work required that she wear it up so she twisted it into a bun on the back. She felt she looked serious and professional at work, yet sweet and sexy, too, and she wore her uniform happily and proudly.

Even in today's horrible crisis, Alana was able to fulfill her mission and didn't let her co-workers down. She was able to put on a brave face and help Jim, even though her heart was pounding.

Since her years in high school, Alana had dreamt of becoming a police officer and doing something heroic, but this goal was not easy for her to attain. She was short of the driving skills and know-how needed to directly enter the Police Academy. All the Police Academy cadets were required to perform 'vehicle operations' at the highest level.

Like every American schoolgirl, Alana had taken a teenage driving course and gotten her license. The problem was she and her mother couldn't afford to buy even a second-hand car, especially with rising gas prices. The car insurance would also be an additional expense beyond their bare-bones budget.

Alana's mother, Maria, didn't drive and didn't need to. She worked at home and took public transport when she went out. Alana had to continue riding her bicycle, which was fine, except in the rain and cold.

As a result of her financial situation, Alana had little chance to practice and strengthen her driving skills and, after several years, had nearly forgotten how to drive.

In spite of this setback, Alana refused to give up and determined to find another route to her dream. She found out it was possible to get a law enforcement job based on two years experience in security work. So that was she found her present position.

Alana easily got the first security job she applied for. No wonder, she was young, strong, athletic and smart. After a short training period, she began working and was now ten months into the job.

Though her salary wasn't impressive, Alana could make ends meet since she lived with her mother. In two more months she would be eligible for a car loan and small salary increase. She figured she would then be able to cover monthly car payments as well as insurance. Owning a car would allow her a chance to practice driving after work and build up her experience. Then, after two years in security, she would be ready to apply to the police.

During her probation period for the security agency, Alana had worked a variety of shifts at a variety of sites, mostly in downtown Minneapolis. For the last few months she had been stuck in the expensive and prestigious St. Boniface Hospital which had proved to be especially quiet and boring. Nothing remarkable at all had happened – until tonight, that is.

Of course, sometimes in the Emergency Department people were rushed in after horrible car accidents or there were drug overdoses, but since they went straight to the Emergency Room, Alana never saw them or met them. She had never worked as a patient watch as the more experienced Jim and Tracy did, and they had never asked for her help before. She was only responsible for the lonely patrolling of the hallways, locking doors, checking alarms and security cameras, monitoring visitors and surveying the parking lot.

Tonight Alana had had her first serious security 'adventure'. It wasn't easy, but she had stood up to the challenge. Now that she'd calmed down and changed her uniform she was ready to resume her usual routine.

Alana left the locker room and began her evening patrol. She needed to check the hospital top floor and then the basement.

One hour later, at the completion of her rounds, she entered the security office on the main floor. There, three of her co-workers were discussing the earlier bloody events. Tracy, a small, middle-aged blonde sat at the computer screen. Jim and Ramesh, an eighteen-year-old East-Indian, were settled down at the table in the center of the room.

"How's that guy doing?" Jim asked Alana as she came in and joined them.

"How should I know? I didn't go back. Maybe he's still sleeping."

Jim went on, "His name is Nick Bell. We are looking him up on the Internet. I was right. He is a millionaire."

Tracy read the screen and then reported, "His father, Gustav Bell, owns the *Astoria*. Do you know the *Astoria* on the South-West?"

5

The other three nodded. Everyone knew the *Astoria,* a five-star, thirty-five-floor hotel.

"...and seven other hotels in Minneapolis and St. Paul," continued Ramesh excitedly. "And three shopping malls. Also two towers at Central Square. And some bowling lines..."

"This idiot, his son, is a lawyer and has an office downtown," Tracy explained, turning round toward Alana and standing up, "plus he owns the *Three Stars Casino.* Can you just imagine how much he makes in one day? Much more than all of us put together in the whole month. Shit!"

"Look! Last year his father bought the *West-Build Management Company,* which owns eight high-rises downtown!" exclaimed Ramesh, who took Tracy's spot in front of the computer and kept on studying Nick Bell's bio.

"Hmmm, *West-Build?*" Alana wrinkled her nose. "I'm sure I've heard something about it...I don't remember what. I better ask my mom. I'm sure she knows something."

"He is thirty-five. No wife or kids. Divorced three years ago," Tracy read over Ramesh's shoulder.

"Maybe that is why he tried to kill himself?" Alana proposed.

"Oh, come on," Jim laughed ironically. "Three years ago, didn't you hear? If it was the divorce it must have been some delayed reaction! Sure as hell, it wasn't that. Probably he's on drugs or gay..."

"That's the kind of problems millionaires specialize in," Tracy added, giving them a wink and everybody chuckled.

Alana felt slightly uncomfortable over the direction of the conversation and the dirty gossipy speculation about Nick Bell's life. She didn't even like the idea of searching the Internet to get the 'low-down' on the man she had seen in such obvious distress a couple of hours earlier. Mr. Bell's case was a serious matter and she didn't feel right making fun of him, even if he was rich. Her curiosity peaked; she decided to go and take a look at him and see how he was doing.

Alana's eyes went to the big clock on the wall. Only ten minutes left until the end of her shift.

"Buy, guys," she said as she went out the office door. "Call the Center, please. I'm off. I'll wait for my relief in the lobby."

"Buy," they all waved to her.

Before heading home, Alana peeked into Cell B to have a quick look at the remarkably miserable man.

Washed, cleaned and dressed in a blue hospital gown, he was lying, covered, on the bed. His wrists were both bandaged tightly and the IV was securely in place. He seemed sound asleep.

6

On her tiptoes, Alana entered his private room and studied his face. He was very pale and his lips were nearly gray. It was difficult to say if he was really breathing or not. She thought he could be described as very handsome, if only he didn't look so much like a corpse.

Alana's heart was moved with pity by the figure in front of her.

My gosh, she thought. It's so sad that he wanted to end his life. Why did he try to do that?

She put her hand on Nick's forehead - it sensed a bit damp and warm. So, he was alive. Alana sighed in relief and felt free to head home now.

She cycled through the streets, enjoying the beauty of the night city. Her shift had ended at midnight and she knew her mother would by this time be asleep. Alana was tired and already saw herself arriving at the underground parking garage where she would leave her bike, take the elevator to the main floor, unlock their apartment and quietly slip into her bedroom without waking her mom.

Tomorrow was her day off. Alana was really looking forward to seeing her boyfriend Tom, a rookie policeman. They had planned to go to the movies together. Just like always, they would eat popcorn, throw the puffy kernels at each other and have a good laugh. Later they would go to their favorite bar, drink beer with their friends and dance a little.

She expected that Tom would again play the toy vending machine in order to get another Winnie the Pooh, or perhaps Tigger, a rabbit or some dog for her. (In truth, her bedroom was already full of these 'trophies' from Tom.) Only then would she tell him the horrible suicide attempt case she had witnessed that night at work.

Later they would end up in Tom's apartment and listen to his CDs and make love. Alana knew that she and Tom were well-matched and very happy together. Jim had been right – life was amazing! Everything was so simple and so clear.

Poor guy, she thought, as her mind drifted back to Nick Bell lying in the hospital. I'm so lucky that I am not a millionaire!

Chapter 2

NICK'S FEELING OF UTTER DISGUST was as bottomless as the universe. It permeated the air and wouldn't leave him. Surrounded by foul and hatred, he felt that there was no escape from it; that he would never be able to cleanse his soul. It was unbearable, absolutely insufferable.

He wanted desperately to end this feeling, to stop breathing, only to slip into unconsciousness. Just to get away from this hell – forever.

Nick lay in the bathtub full of warm water too agitated to relax. Abruptly he reversed the tap to hot and, at the same time, picked up his razor. He had thought about it enough. It was the only way to block the raging pain in his soul, to take away the total despair he felt.

He slashed his left wrist first, then switched hands and cut his right veins, as well. It wasn't scary and, he was surprised, it wasn't even painful. Soon the water began turning red as the blood slowly diffused. Nick watched it first, stupefied, but then he closed his eyes and drifted into the abyss.

In rays of sunshine his mother's image floated down from the sky and reached out to him. He had almost forgotten what she looked like. She had died of cancer when he was only sixteen but now Nick saw her face clearly and felt her warmth embracing him. It brought peace and quiet just to see her so bright and loving.

"Mom," he whispered to her. She smiled instead of answering.

Nick stretched his arms out to hug her, but she eluded him. It was strange – she was so close, however, at the same time very far away. Then his mother turned and drifted back to the sun in the sky. Nick floated after her.

The apparition melted and in its place Nick saw the steady and stern face of his father, emerging out of the dark mist. He heard once again his father's strong voice, just as he spoke six month after the burial. "Our mourning is finished today. It's time to return to normal life, son. Let's talk about business."

Gustav Bell didn't consider Nick's tender age and feelings. He had great expectations for his only son. He needed a helper in his business and Nick was the one to shoulder this responsibility.

"I know that your grades at school are pretty good and you're a very smart guy," Gustav Bell explained. "You've had enough schooling. It's all arranged. You'll go to university, to Harvard, and study business management and law. I need my own business partner and my own lawyer. I can't trust anyone but family. Everyone else is a liar and a cheat. You and I have one business and one family purse. All that I have – now and in the future – will be yours. You know that. All my hopes are on you now, my son. I'll train you and help you. Your only job is to listen to me."

Nick had always loved and respected his father. That he had earned the trust of such a successful businessman as Gustav Bell made him feel very proud, indeed. He was happy and enthusiastic to follow his father's advice and instructions and he took the conversation very seriously.

By nature a romantic, Nick took after his affectionate mother. She was very talented poetess of Russian heritage and had raised him to appreciate classical literature, music and art. He grew to truly love them, while the world of business – his father's world – reminded alien to him. As a matter of fact, Gustav Bell had seldom paid any attention to his son or talked to him about business before.

To Nick's inexperienced mind, businessmen were proud and independent and wore the best suits, shoes and watches. They also drove the most expensive cars, enjoyed splendid wines and cigars, not to mention the most beautiful women in the world. As far as he could see, they did little else, except maybe for some work-out at the most prestigious fitness clubs in order to stay in shape.

The hard work required and the round-the-clock responsibility needed to maintain a successful business was beyond his teenage mentality.

"Sure, Dad," Nick whispered filled with excitement. "Of course, I'll listen and study. I'll become a businessman and a lawyer. Thanks so much for your faith in me. I promise I'll do everything you ask."

Pained to the point of tears, Nick now thought back and realized how totally naïve, inexperienced and childish he had been in his grasp of business.

Then a third familiar face slowly appeared before Nick. It was his long-time best friend, Gary Edwards, whom he had first met at Harvard. Gary, a dark-haired, blue-eyed intellectual, was an active and careful young man, very frank and open.

Their nearly twelve years together at Harvard University had sealed their close friendship. They not only had in common the same hobbies and interests, sat together in lectures, did their homework side by side and shared secrets, but even dated girls who were sisters or close friends. The whole university saw them constantly together and knew that Nick

Bell and Gary Edwards were the best friends imaginable. Unlike many maturing men their friendship even grew stronger over the years.

Yet Nick and Gary were from two contrasting backgrounds. Nick disregarded the gap between the social standing of their families. He saw no problem with Gary's father working as a simple high school mathematics teacher.

Gary was three years Nick's senior and had already began to make his mark in the world. He was a winner of all Math Olympiads in his home state of North Carolina, which led to his partial college scholarship. For the rest of his expenses, Gary took out a college loan from the bank and sometimes delivered pizza for extra spending money.

Nick's father, Gustav, of course, paid in full for his son's education, but Nick enjoyed helping Gary deliver pizzas just for the fun of it.

Even over Thanksgiving, Christmas and Easter holidays, the young men were inseparable; together they would visit first one family in Minneapolis and then the other in Raleigh.

"I don't really like Gary," Nick's dad once told him privately. "You aren't coming from the same place. I'm sure he wants to get something from you. He is probably using you – or will in the future."

"In what way?" Nick laughed at such an absurd idea. "He isn't gay and he's never borrowed money from me – not even a penny. Sure, I help him with his homework and his exams, but we are friends and I like to see him do well. He helps me in many ways, too."

"In what ways?" his father demanded.

"Well, for one, he is my friend, and he saves me from boredom and loneliness. For another he has a perfect sense of humor and we laugh a lot together. With him I always have a good time."

"Well," said the senior Bell, shrugging his shoulders and making a face. "Just remember I warned you."

However, there was one clear major difference between the two young men. Nick was driven to take over his father's business and open a law office, but Gary was motivated not by the business and law he was studying, but rather to become a rich and famous writer.

"No business can bring you more money that writing a bestseller," he always said. "I just need to find something to write about – a great idea – and to develop my talent."

It was ironic that Gary, brilliant in math and gifted in sports, had absolutely no writing talent at all. When he wrote anything (from a Christmas card to a poem for someone's birthday) his prose and verse were graceless, dull, and plodding. Nick usually stepped in and patched up Gary's writing and helped it to sing. Nick felt at home with writing.

It was easy for him. He had inherited a great deal of talent from his cultured mother, but had never seriously considered himself a writer. It was just an enjoyable hobby for him.

Gary's lack of skill in the writing department, on the contrary, caused him irritation and mild depression. He unconsciously stuck to Nick, hoping to learn from him that was the underlying reason of his friendship. Gary hopefully thought that talent could be learned and earned by exercise.

As he now reflected on his past, Nick was painfully struck by his youthful trust and naivety. How blind he had been so long!

Complete darkness descended upon Nick, blacking out Gary's face.

This is probably the end, he thought, and with that he relaxed into a stupor.

Nick felt quite content with the blank before him, but then came Laura's image. He was not happy to see her appear, but suddenly her Barbie-doll looks and fountain of golden hair arose from his past. Nick faced her seemingly innocent blue eyes.

Five years ago as he met her, he could find no trace of thought or feeling in the emptiness of her eyes expression. He could only sense himself drowning in that vast nothingness, like in the ocean of love.

When Nick had announced to his father that he wanted to get married, Gustav Bell wholeheartedly approved.

"I've been expecting that," he said. "It's high time you had a wife. Your law office is successful. You are off to a good start in business. It would be benefit for your public image if you showed up at meetings and presentations with strikingly beautiful Missis. It often helps. Your partners and associates will feel more drawn to you. And they'll trust you more."

It wasn't long before Nick found Laura Adams at a beauty pageant. She had just won the title of 'Miss Minnesota'. He had reached the age of thirty, but she was a fresh eighteen-year-old, a real live Barbie. Of course other, and richer men, were pursuing her as well. In the end, Nick beat out several others because he was young and charming, as well as suitable wealthy.

From 'Miss Minnesota' Laura went to the 'Miss America' competition. She put him off, hoping to win the national crown, but it was much tougher and she even failed to place. This set off her bad temper, and, in her anger she damaged some furniture in her hotel room in Atlantic City. It took a month for her to fully calm down and when she did, she consented to become Mrs. Bell.

Nick's father pulled out all the stops with a grand Minneapolis wedding and honeymoon in Rome. Laura talked Nick into putting a red Ferrari F-360 Spider convertible in their triple garage just for her.

The groom was totally in love with his beauty queen. None of his past girlfriends could hold a candle to Laura's style, grace and sex appeal. Although she was more silly than serious and had little to converse about, not for one minute did Nick hesitate to marry her. If he needed intellectual stimulation or savvy advice he could always go to his father. There was also Gary, who had followed him back to Minnesota and worked with him in the law office. He also had many professional colleagues on his level.

So lovely Laura was his wife and provided him with quality sex. Not only she did easily turn him on, but she was more than willing and satisfying every time. What more could he ask for to make him happy? At thirty, Nick believed he was on top of the world – and understood life pretty well.

Thinking back, miserably, to those days Nick cursed his own stupidity and simple-mindedness to lovingly trust Laura the way he did.

One day his wife brought home a little gray kitten. Nick wasn't very happy about it.

"Are you sure it won't scratch the furniture?" he asked her.

"Don't worry. I'll take him to the vet and have him de-clawed," Laura assured him. "That way I won't get scratched either. When cats get excited they usually sink their claws into everything."

Several months later, Nick noticed the young cat sleeping on the couch with bandaged paws and realized the surgery had been completed, but it barely registered with him. It didn't matter much to him how Laura managed to entertain herself. She needed something to do while he was busy at work. It was clear that she loved her growing kitten, talking to it like a child. She had refused to get pregnant, claiming that she was still too young and wanted more time to herself.

She is probably right, Nick thought. The cat can fill her life for now. And he left her alone.

Cats...Millions of people all over the world have cats as pets! He didn't really see anything wrong with it at the time. Who would?

Not long after, a small, smelly bottle, containing a tincture of valerian appeared in the medicine cabinet. Nick noticed that the odor overpowered all of Laura's perfumed shampoos and body oils. The disgusting scent filled the whole master bathroom, where the small bottle sat next to Laura's birth control pills.

"What's that smell?" Nick demanded, with a pained expression on his face.

"Oh, this? It's just a treat for the cat. I like to spoil him sometimes," Laura said with a laugh. "I'll show you. Watch this."

She took the valerian stopper out of the bottle and put a couple drops on the dark green marble bathroom floor.

With the first full whiff, the furry figure suddenly appeared, jumped to the spot and began licking the valerian like a crazed animal. Growling wildly, the cat's tongue continued lapping the clean, wet marble long after the tiny spot had been removed.

"That's crazy!" Nick exclaimed. He'd never seen anything like it. "Is it going to lick a hole in the floor?"

"He can carry on that for hours," Laura explained. "It's amazing to see, isn't it?"

Nick gently picked up the cat and tried to pull it away from the spot. The little body resisted him fiercely. He was startled to feel how tense the cat's stomach muscles were under the soft gray down. Its tummy was as hard as a rock. All this time, the cat continued growling and trying to claw its way out with its de-fanged paws. It was a pitiful, crazy scene and not at all to Nick's liking.

"Okay, you can do whatever you like," Nick said gruffly. "Just wrap the bottle somehow. It really stinks to high heaven!"

Maybe Laura had done what he asked because the valerian smell disappeared and Nick forgot all about it. He had enough more important things on his mind.

The cat…It was unbelievable how much he hated cats now. He had once considered them cute little things. Laura's gray cat with a white muzzle, wet pink nose, big green eyes and rough pink tongue had changed all that.

The cat was about a year-and-a-half when it happened. Like the old-heard story, the husband comes home early from work and finds his wife with her lover. Now Nick thought if it had only been a rival lover, he could have handled it.

That warm summer afternoon, Nick dropped by the house to pick up Laura on his way to a meeting. He knew she planned to be home all day so he didn't bother to phone first. When he parked his Mercedes in the driveway, he noticed the bedroom window was open. The delicate lace curtains were quivering in the breeze. As he walked to the front door, he could hear Laura's moans coming from the window. He couldn't quite tell if the sound came from passion, a strange laughter or even pain. He knew that she sometimes suffered from horrible migraines.

Nick entered the house and dashed up the stairs three at a time to the master bedroom.

The double doors were slightly ajar and he quietly opened one into the bedroom he and Laura shared every night. Even though the windows were wide open, the room was drenched in the odor of valerian and it become clear why. What Nick witnessed put him in deep shock and he rigidly stood on the threshold.

Spread-eagled on the luscious raspberry-colored silk sheets was his naked wife. Her long, slender, well-tanned legs were opened with her pet cat positioned between. Serving as her surrogate lover, it licked her pussy again and again, and kneaded her thighs with its thick velvety paws. Laura was writhing with ecstasy underneath the pink, rough tongue, adding her shrieks and sobs to cat's growls. The woman and her pet – pussy and pussy – were so wrapped up in each other they didn't even notice Nick was here.

For at least five minutes he stood in the doorway trying not to see what he was clearly seeing before him. His wife's moral lapse was the last thing he had ever expected to witness.

Nick would never in a thousand years have thought this possible. It paralyzed his brain to see such degradation of his family, his house and his marital bed. He was stupefied, choked and immobile. If he hadn't been such a young, healthy man he might easily have been affected by a heart attack on the spot. A sharp spasm tightened his throat. It took all his strength to hold himself in check.

How could she do that? Nick's first thought was. Then, but, why? Don't I satisfy her? It is certain that she had never shown so much passion in bed with me.

That thought alone produced a devastating blow to his male pride. He was suffering the most humiliating shock in the world.

What could be worse than this? Even another male lover would be better, he believed.

It was just too insulting to take. The level of outrage he felt was so intense that it could only be washed away by blood. Something deep inside called him to kill right there and then. Nick trembled and shook, about to erupt, like a volcano.

"Laura!! What the hell are you doing?!" he screamed at her as he jumped onto the bed.

She looked up, as did the startled cat. Quickly Nick seized the offending pet by the scruff of the neck and tore it away from his wife's body. In three steps he was at the open window and with the force of utter rage, hurtled the small beast against the trunk of the elm tree in the yard. As the cat hit the tree it screeched and sought to embed its claws into the bark but, failing, slid down onto the sharp edge of the garage roof instead. The impact brook the poor cat's spine and it dropped, lifeless into a pool of blood in the driveway in front of his car.

Laura jumped up in bed, infuriated.

"What the hell are YOU doing?" she yelled at Nick, wrapping herself in her chiffon peignoir. "Son of a bitch, you robbed me of my orgasm. And what have you done to Puffy?"

She ran to the window and surveyed the scene below.

"Oh, Puffy!" she cried in horror and tried to run downstairs to the rescue. Nick blocked her exit, grabbed her by the shoulders and threw her back onto the bed.

"Why did you do it?" he shouted in pained despair. "Why? Tell me why?"

Sitting in the tub now, Nick heard his question as it were an echo in dark eternity. The sound spread round him endlessly like electronic music.

"Why?" he had asked. Well, it didn't matter anymore what Laura had answered. It didn't even matter that they had fearsome fights after that that bruised more than his ego. And it didn't matter to him that Laura promised to revenge her dead feline playmate.

She was no longer his wife – or his woman. He found it impossible to love, look at or even talk to her anymore. It seemed that she was deader that the cat, and his feelings for her also ceased to exist.

Laura, bent on vengeance, tried to further inflict damage on Nick. However, there was really nothing more she could do to punish him than what she had already done to destroy his world.

Some days, Laura would drive around in her convertible until she found a filthy homeless vagrant on the streets to pick up. For kicks she would hire him, bring him home and stage a sex show with the unwashed stranger in front of Nick in their bedroom.

Laura was position herself down on all fours on the edge of the bed, while the dirty man from behind would be fucking her with a victorious cackle. His gigantic fingers with their soiled broken nails would be squeezing her charming ass and bulbous tits for all he was worth.

Nick, now indifferent to these antics performed for his behalf, shrugged his shoulders, turned, walked into his study and shut the door. Through it, though, he could still hear her mad shrieks and the vagrant's crude grunts. Nick finally dialed the police calmly and requested that they remove this crazy couple from his private property. The police responded immediately and kicked out the dirty scum.

"I'll go with him!" Laura exclaimed passionately, hanging on her new boyfriend's neck. "He's much better fucker that you, idiot! Baaaah!" she made a face and showed her long pink tongue to Nick.

It took her only fifteen minutes to gather her belongings and get out. Nick didn't react. She had failed to get her pound of flesh.

Laura didn't give up easily, however. Her creativity was bent to her twisted purpose and she would return to the North-West Blooms district where Nick's home stood. She would slowly cruise up and down the street in her red Ferrari with her homeless 'friend' hanging on her. In front of each neighbor's home they would begin to make out passionately. Again, the mindless vagrant giggled happily while Laura with all of her exhibitionist flair encouraged him to open up her low-cut sundress and publicly fondle her nubile breasts while she cooed.

This crass demonstration was fatal to Nick's professional reputation. Understandably the whole neighborhood was shocked and disgusted by such scenes, carried out by a member of their own social class 'gone over the edge'. The gossip flew fast from one wag to another and the Bell social 'stock' dropped lower every day. The neighbors were so mortified that they made sure it stayed out of the city news – at least for the time being.

To save face Nick was forced to act to salvage the business and what was left of his personal life. He had reached the end of the line.

Nick discussed the problem with Gary but still feared to put it before his father.

Then Laura phoned him.

"Do you want me to stop my little show?" she asked shamelessly. "Well, it will only cost you five million dollars. Just hand me the check and I will disappear from your life."

"I can't possibly raise such a large amount of money without my father's agreement," Nick admitted. "You should just make an appointment with him."

This was the moment when Gustav Bell was supposed to step in. It was very difficult for Nick to bring up such a painful and personal matter with his father. When he broached the subject, Nick was braced for an outburst of accusation but he was greatly surprised by his dad's common sense response.

"Hmmm," the elder Bell said thoughtfully. "It's partly my fault, I suppose. I advised you to marry a beauty. On second thought it was probably better to choose someone shy and romantic, more like your mother. But I found that that didn't help my business at all. Now we can see that beauty doesn't work to our benefit, either. You know, it's hard to figure woman out. Anyway, Nick, you have to free yourself from her as quickly as possible. The last thing we want is a real scandal over this. Ask her to come to my office. I'll deal with her, all right."

When Laura arrived for her appointment she took an aggressive stance with her father-in-law. She was playing a risky game and she concluded that the best defense was to attack. So she began shouting about Nick's rude behavior and attempts to curb her 'sexual freedom'.

"I'll keep pushing him into the dirt," she declared insolently, "until I get my five million!"

Even though Gustav Bell was a serious, educated and responsible man he soon lost patience with this outrageous 'beauty queen'. Holding the check in one hand, he grabbed the demanding gold digger with the other on the collar of her blouse, twisted it almost strangling her and drew her close to his face. Then nose-to-nose he hissed at her, "One million, you little bitch! Otherwise I'll hire someone to take care of you and you'll disappear in cement down in some construction hole forever!"

When he finally loosened his grip, Laura chocked, gasping for breath. It only took a second for her to snatch the check, however, and run out of the office on her stiletto hills. In a short time the divorce was legally finalized.

Nick's home in North-West Blooms was immediately sold and he relocated to a smaller and more modest home in Twins South.

Why did all of this happen? Nick wrestled with this question for months on end. He stopped asking why his wife chose a cat as a lover or why she turned into a sexual sick-o after a year-and-a-half of what he thought was a happy marriage. Most likely even the best psychiatrist would have trouble answering those.

He just wanted to know why fate had handed him that particular plate. What did he do to deserve it? The old 'Why me, Lord?' question.

Through all of this stress and anguish Nick found that Gary was always there for him. Not only was he understanding and offered to carry the heaviest load at the law office, he also advised Nick to get some professional help to work through everything. The psychologist he found did prove to be very helpful. They talked over the entire courtship and marriage and concluded that it was a loveless relationship from the start.

Sure, Nick had felt sexual attraction for Laura and enjoyed the prestige of wedding a beauty, but clearly, Laura had only been after money. This was the ugly part that Nick finally had to admit to himself. However, in confessing his failure, Nick couldn't find a way out of his cul-de-sac. How could he possibly purify his heart and soul and return to a normal life? Could he ever be a whole and healthy man again?

"You have to keep a journal," the psychologist suggested. "Paper is like a magnet. It sucks up all the emotions and stresses from the author. You just pour it all out onto paper, everything that robs you of peace of mind. When you finish, you will feel cleansed and free again. This sordid chapter of your life will be behind you and forgotten forever. Then you can start a new life."

It sounded good and not to hard to do. So Nick began writing for his treatment. He spent about two or three hours every night before he retired to get everything down. Long-hand was best. That way he felt his blood flowed through the pen as ink to the page.

Continuing to be so close with Gary, Nick was soon sharing pages with him. Gary suggested that Nick should take the journal notes and shape them into a fictionalized story.

"That way," Gary said, "you'll work through the plot and characters to the climatic end and to form a book."

He was supportive and compassionate about the Nick's chapters he read, but could offer very little in the way of critique or improvements.

As Gary read the growing text he only marveled at its quality. "It's just amazing, Nick. What a wonderful story you tell! You don't even understand what you have here. You are the goose that lays the golden eggs. I predict that you will be fantastically rich and famous someday."

Nick couldn't see what Gary was getting so carried away by. The praise meant little to him. He would have preferred that his friend would give him more practical advice on writing, but that was beyond Gary's expertise.

Still, little by little Nick became fascinated with the process of writing such a personal book. It took him about two years to complete and he lived with it daily. He grew to love the pages he had written as they took form, and the manuscript grew to become his child. It held the meaning of his life.

Nick was so preoccupied with this process that he failed to pay attention when Gary began to refer to it as 'their book'. "We are writing the book," he would say sometimes, or "We are almost finished with our book." Nick hardly noticed these little telling remarks. From his view point, Gary – his closest, loyal friend – was overwhelmed by the tragic love story and the setting down of it.

The day Nick finished the book the two of them celebrated over glasses of whiskey.

"Well, I've done it!" Nick said proudly to Gary. "You might not believe me, but the treatment worked. By writing everything out, I've gotten my own soul back. Now I'm ready to start anew. I'll pour myself into dad's business and, of course, get beck to doing my share in the law firm. I've found a new happiness."

"It's time to think about publishing your baby now," Gary prompted ed him mindfully.

"Oh, it's not important. I didn't write to publish it. Even if it would sell well, I don't need the money. My goal was completely different. And I reached it. You know," Nick looked at Gary, "I treasure this book a lot. It really is my 'baby'. It's my life and my soul on every page. Oh, maybe someday I'll print a few copies for myself, you and a few friends. But that's all."

"Thank you, buddy," Gary said gratefully, embracing his friend.

Three month later, Nick got a surprise phone call from his father. "Did you hear that your friend Gary has published a book?"

"No," Nick found the very idea amazing. "Where did you hear it?"

Gustav Bell explained, "My secretary just saw him on TV a half-an-hour ago. He has being interviewed about his novel. I guess it was the bestselling book of the month. They rated him as potentially the most talented writer of the twenty-first century. How could you best friend author a book and you don't know anything about it? I was wondering, is it possibly YOUR book he published under his own name?"

Nick just couldn't digest what his father was saying. Gary is an author? Gary is pirating his book? They both seemed not only ridiculous, but also impossible! Surely there was some mistake somewhere. It sounded like a mix-up to him.

I'll call Gary and clear this up right away, he thought.

He dialed the home number but there was no answer. So Nick drove to the office, but Gary wasn't working late. Something was strange because Gary never just disappeared from the radar screen.

Suspicion began to creep into Nick's mind though his first impulse was to stick up for his friend. Maybe something underhanded had been going on behind his back. Something he had completely overlooked.

Then, at evening, as Nick was watching TV, he saw Gary with a national talk-show host and a panel of literary critics.

"How did you come up with the idea for your book, Mr. Edwards?"

"How long did it take you to write *My Obsessive Passion*?"

"Where did you character prototypes come from?"

"Is the amazing story of Rick, his wife Nora and the cat based on reality at all?"

"Your father is a teacher. Did you inherit your talent from him?"

"No writer in the past decade has expressed so much passion in his writing as you do, Mr. Edwards. Did you personally survive such misery yourself?"

"The critics are hailing you as a new Ernest Hemingway. What do you think of that?"

For Nick, now sick to his stomach, the voices missed in a muddled blur. They sounded like a distant echo in his aching head. There was so-called his friend Gary, with a smug and mean-spirited expression on his face. This was a side of Gary that had been hidden from him for seventeen years. Nick wondered did he really know Gary at all.

It come to him, that he had been incredibly careless and trusting. When Gary asked him for the disk with manuscript on it, Nick had jokingly told him, "No, your eyes will get tired trying to read it." He never once asked his partner and best friend, "Why do you want it?"

Without the disk, Nick now understood that Gary had to work a little harder to steal the book. He was forced to scan the hard copy pages one by one, or have his secretary do it for him. Besides, he had to change some names and details throughout so as not to be too obvious. Nick's leading character was tall; Gary's was short. The wife was blonde and slim in the original and now she appeared as a shapely brunette; even the cat passed into Siamese, and so it went.

Nick had never taken seriously his friend's dream of being transformed into a famous writer. After it became obvious, that Gary had no talent whatsoever in that direction, Nick's own book arrived on the scene, well-written and tempting. Disregarding their long-standing friendship and the trust Nick had placed in him Gary easily took the creative fruit of his friend's soul and life, titled *My Wildfire Life*. Gary not only kidnapped the 'book-child' but he passed it off as his own.

For Nick this was a total betrayal. Once again his life was in shambles and his heart was ripped out of him.

A year of lawsuits followed. Though Nick hired a good lawyer he was unable to prove anything. Sure, he had a handwritten draft of his manuscript and had a saved copy on his computer. He even had a hard copy with Gary's own notes, scrabbled on it. However, Nick had not copyrighted the material and the Gary's alterations allowed the jury to pronounce *My Obsessive Passion* by Gary Edwards a substantially different book that *My Wildfire Life* by Nick Bell.

The lawsuits and the media exposure put Gary's book in the spotlight and served to sell it better. Thirty million copies were bought during the first months of the year. Nick fired Gary from his office, but Gary didn't need a day job any longer; he had become *the rich and famous writer* he had dreamt of.

At this point he cynically called Nick to rub it in.

"You see, Nicky-old buddy," Gary intoned. "I am the star. Now anything I write – any rubbish, any silly story, and any artless trash – will sell and I will make millions because of my world-famous name. I am 'Gary Edwards' now, and I am very popular. And what are you, Nicky-baby? Nothing. A regular office rat!

"You know, I've always resented you for your gifts, your luck, money and happiness. But just look now. I've got it all! You should understand that justice is not only blind – but dumb, too. I studied law so I could have the tools to win. And guess what! I'm a real winner! Not like you."

Nick said nothing and hung up silently after this outburst from Gary. He felt as though he were being smothered. His heart ached horribly and a wave of nausea washed over his dizzy head.

His three-year-old sickness rushed back in, filling every cavity of his being. The old questions pounding in his head were now joined with a few new ones. How come my best friend stab me like this? Why? Why is this happening to me? Am I just a stupid schmuck, or something? Did I do something terrible to deserve all this? Millions of people own cats! Millions of people write books! Why is everything turning out so badly for me? WHY?

As terrifying as the questions were, the answer which come to him was far more terrifying: he didn't deserve to live in this world. Clearly there was no room for the likes of him. Maybe he was TOO nice. Or TOO unlucky. He should never have been born.

Nick felt totally abandoned and alone. What could he possibly believe in? Could he ever trust again? Was love only a cruel joke or could there ever be such a thing in his life? What was friendship? What was justice? What was life? When the shit hits the fan, everyone is forced to be a philosopher. Nick was full of aching despair. What was the point of living?

Now, sitting at the bloody bathtub, Nick slowly sunk into an eternal dream, finally escaping the last question. He slept down; his head threw back and fell on the edge of the tub. The water dripped on the floor. Nick found it difficult to breathe as he saw one more apparition in front of his eyes in the darkness.

He saw himself at his last minutes before the suicide – minutes of his final decision. He was sitting motionless on the couch, standing at gaze on Gary's book on his coffee table.

My own book with the thief's name on it, he thought.

Opening to the dedication page, Nick scribbled a harsh letter to Gary. Then he left the book on his desk in the study, abruptly went to the bathroom, filled the tub with warm water and took out a razor.

He felt like a worthless worm, unable to justify taking up space in this overcrowded world. In fact, it had turned into Laura and Gary's world and he couldn't stand it any longer. He'd clearly lost the game of life so it was time for his exit.

The golden cover of *My Obsessive Passion* depicting a dead cat in a puddle of blood was the last thing that floated in Nick's mind before he passed out.

Suddenly a terrible scream pierced the darkness of the farthest reaches of Nick's unconscious mind. Bob and Mary Johns, Nick's live-in caretakers downstairs, discovered the pink liquid dripping through their ceiling from the master bedroom. Bob immediately ran upstairs and knocked loudly on the bathroom door. There was no answer, only the sound of running water which was seeping out into the hall, as well. Bob opened the unlocked door a crack.

"Oh, my God! Mr. Bell! Nick!" he yelled in horror. "Mary, Mary, call an ambulance right away! Hurry up! Please, dear God! Maybe it's not too late!"

Then Bob tore his handkerchief in strips and bound Nick's bloody wrists as tightly as he could.

Chapter 3

THE NEXT DAY, ALANA'S SUPERVISOR called her to ask if she could take over Tracy's shifts in patient watch for the following two weeks. Alana felt uncomfortable about the unexpected request. She preferred her present duties to patient watch, especially now. After the last suicide attempt case she didn't care to see anything like that again.

However, she really had no choice in the matter. Following the Security Code of Ethics, guards were allowed to swap shifts with one another. Sometimes Alana's co-workers took her shifts when she went to a cabin at the lake with Tom or traveled with him on his motorcycle to see his parents in Duluth. Of course, it was expected that she return the favor.

When Alana arrived at St. Boniface's for Tracy's shift, she peered into Cell B and discovered that Nick Bell wasn't there.

"Was he discharged?" she asked the duty nurse who had been in the room that fateful night.

"Oh, no," the nurse shook her head. "He's still around. He has been transferred to the third floor, room 301. He came out of surgery where his wrists were stitched. He needed a lot of donor blood. You'll have to stay with him all the time because the doctor isn't sure he won't try something again. He's still mentally unstable. But if he should become aggressive, you should immediately call for help."

This wasn't welcome news. Alana felt anxious about the situation she was entering, but she pulled herself together and put a brave face on it. She had to, if she ever expected to be a police officer someday.

Nick was sleeping, the IV connected firmly to his arm. There was a little more color in his face now - the cheeks and lips had returned to normal shades. His eyes were still ringed with dark circles, but the breathing was calm. It was clear that he was recovering and his life was no longer in danger.

Alana gazed at him intently. He had blonde wavy hair with dark brows and long eyelashes. The unshaven bristle on his jaw line looked much darker than his hair. As she studied his face she decided that he was attractive, even manly.

Such a handsome man, Alana thought. It would be interesting to look into his eyes to know him better. It seems that he had been given everything in life. Yet, clearly, something was missing. What was he lacking? I would like to understand. I just know that I could never commit suicide myself. Nothing could ever drive me to that point.

She restlessly wandered around the room for awhile; then settled down to read a magazine in an armchair beside the bed in the private room.

About two hours passed and the patient was still sleeping. Alana decided she would take her lunch break and radioed Jim to relieve her. She went to the hospital cafeteria on the fourth floor, had a simple meal of soup and salad and joked with two nurses and a new young doctor sitting at her table. Alana returned to room 301, happy and smiling.

She was bewildered to see Jim leaning over the patient and gesturing for her to be quiet.

"Shhh," Jim whispered to her. "He's saying something."

Alana approached the bed. "What's he saying? I don't hear anything."

"He called for somebody named Gary and said he was the bastard who stole his baby."

"Oh, my," Alana noted in hushed voice. "That's *why* he did it! It's horrible if someone steals your baby. He should have called the police if he knew who took him." Then, with a puzzled look on her face, remembered, "You told me he didn't have any kids, didn't you?"

Jim shrugged, "That's what it said on the Internet. Who knows? Maybe the situation changed. Everything there is not always up-to-date. Anyone can have a baby just like that," Jim snapped his fingers and chuckled. "Okay, I have to go. Just listen carefully if he talks again. I'll be interested what else this guy's got to say. Okay?"

Alana nodded and returned to her chair and magazine. Some time had passed when she felt a pair of eyes on her. She looked up and saw Nick Bell gazing at her; his eyes were green and hot.

"Hi," Alana ventured and gave him a little smile. "How are you doing? Everything okay?"

"Are you guarding me?" he queried, not bothering to answer her question. "Why?"

"Because you weren't feeling well. But now you are better, I hope."

Nick looked toward the window. He could make out the branches of a huge elm tree quivering in the wind, creating a latticed pattern of sun and shade on the white curtains of his room.

"It's a sunny day," he commented dolefully. "I'm in the hospital, aren't I?"

"Yeah," Alana confirmed.

"Why am I here?" Nick wanted to know.

"An ambulance brought you here a couple of days ago."

"Who called them?" Nick began coughing, because his mouth was dry after days of silence. "It's strange... No one was at home..."

He sounded weak and confused, looking helplessly around the room.

"I'd better call the nurse," Alana said, placing her magazine on the table and walking out.

When she returned an hour later, Nick had been shaved, changed and fed. The head of the bed had been raised to support him in a sitting position. He shot Alana a sheepish smile.

"Oh, I see you are better," Alana told him kindly and sat near the bed.

"I'm so full of medication that I feel as a happy idiot," Nick confessed simply, like she was his old friend. "I've never spent time in the hospital before, you know. Never really been sick. Even now I'm not sick...I'm more frustrated and had to kill someone..." he paused, looking for the right words, "...who was not wanted in this world."

"Why do you think you are not wanted?" Alana asked.

"Why?" he repeated sarcastically. "It's my favorite question. Why? That's what I'm trying my best to understand. I think it's because I saw meanness, betrayal and injustice, my dear young lady. I felt the full force of them personally. They were real feelings from real events. When I found myself surrounded by a dirty world, I didn't want to live anymore. But, thanks to these medications, I don't really care one way or the other. I can't say how long I will feel this way, though."

"You should want to live," Alana told him sincerely. "I believe so. It doesn't matter what happened in your life. You know, I'm not a religious person, so let's say that Nature created all of us. So, we have to continue living, because it's the natural thing to do. We have no right to end our lives until they end naturally."

Nick gave her an ironic smile. "What about accidents?" he asked.

"An accident is an accident; it's fate. You can't prevent it. They happen suddenly and unconsciously."

"Well, then, I had an accident – a mental accident. I crashed into malice and villainy *suddenly and unconsciously*, as you say. Even worse though, I tried to fight them for an entire year and I was defeated. Injustice was victorious on top of all that I suffered! So, you could say that I was the victim of a tragic accident, too. And my life was over as far as I was concerned."

"You did it to yourself!" Alana objected heatedly. "Nature gave us – you and me – a really big bonus: good health. Do you know how many people in this hospital alone are dying of cancer, MS and bad hearts? I'm absolutely sure that anyone of them would be happy to trade places with you. Their dream is to live longer.

"You must try," she continued, "to put yourself in their shoes. Just imagine how they feel. My mother taught me to empathize with others when, as a kid, I used to tear the wings off dragonflies and butterflies or pulled the tails of pappies."

"Well, my mother taught me the same lesson," Nick retorted. "I can imagine that all those sick and dying people are unhappy, but I'm not convinced they would have survived what I went through. If they had, they wouldn't want to go on living – and they would see their illness as a blessing that will end the pain."

"Not necessarily," Alana objected. "Okay, let's leave the sick people out of it. Let's look at people who are healthy, but had encountered meanness, betrayal and…"

"Injustice!" Nick reminded her.

"And injustice. I haven't experienced them myself but I know that my father was killed at age forty and that was both unfair and cruel. I never knew him at all. I was born after he died. My mother immigrated to the U.S. before she even knew she was pregnant."

"Oh, were she was from?" Nick inquired. "You don't sound like a foreigner."

"Of course not. I was born here in Minneapolis. I'm an American. But my parents were German. They tried to escape the Communist regime of East Germany. They were fleeing to the West over the Berlin Wall, when my father was shot by Russian border guards. It was terrible."

"I could imagine…"

"No, you couldn't. Sure, you've seen Cold War movies and all but this was more than just a thriller. I know this story from my mom and I know all that she had to survive. My father dreamt to live, to be free and have a family. They loved each other dearly. Of course she was devastated when she lost him, but she never once considered committing suicide. She thought only about her future life and raising me. I'm really proud of my parents: they are my heroes," Alana was caught up in the passion of her beliefs.

"If you think about people like that," she advised to Nick, "you will begin to understand the value of life. You have to live for their sake. It's your duty!"

"Your mother had a future in you," Nick objected, staring at Alana with new interest. This girl was quite unusual, not your typical security guard at all. "But I had no future before me."

"Do you mean your baby?"

"My baby?" Nick couldn't understand what she was talking about.

Now Alana was confused, too. "Yes," she nodded. She felt uncomfortable asking personal questions but she still had a burning curiosity about Nick. "You were talking in your sleep this afternoon. You murmured that someone stole your baby."

"Did I?" Nick broke into a bitter smile. "It's these strong medications they're giving me. I never talked in my sleep before. Anyway, 'my baby' isn't about child at all. It's about my book – I poured my whole soul in it and it holds the meaning of my existence."

"Oh. Are you a writer?"

"No, not really. It's difficult to explain. My story is very long and probably boring for a young lady like you. I doubt that you would want to hear it."

"But I would," Alana affirmed without hesitation. She was amazed that a handsome and rich man would speak to her so openly and trustingly. She had never met anyone on his level before and would have expected him to be arrogant and snobbish, but he wasn't like that at all. Nick seemed to be open, sincere and accessible, much to her relief.

Nick, himself, was relieved to be able to share heart-to-heart. He had forgotten the last time he had talked to someone confidentially. It had probably been Gary, over a year ago.

Yet Nick, for all of his writing ability, wasn't the best storyteller of the two. During their university dating days, it was usually Gary who would charm and entertain the girls they went out with, with jokes and stories. Later, as he was forming his book, Nick gained experience and confidence and now could talk for hours. This was especially true of his life story and personal tragedy. He began telling Alana about his early childhood and his earliest memories.

She was a good listener. It was her job now, in fact, to listen to crazy patients in the hospital. Still, she also took pleasure in the trust that Nick, a good-looking and inscrutable man, placed in her. She looked on him and felt closer as he revealed more about himself.

Unfortunately, Alana's shift ended before the whole story was told, so they continued their conversation over the following days. The only breaks they took were when a nurse or doctor entered to check on Nick, or when his father arrived for a visit.

27

It took about a week of detailed recollections for Nick to reach the point where Laura had brought the cat home. He then broke off the account.

"What the matter?" Alana wanted to know.

"You seem to be my friend and understand a lot about me," Nick admitted, "but, still, there are some things I can't really tell you. I've got an idea. I think it would be okay if you read my book; it explains everything much better than I can tell you."

"Okay. If you think that is best."

"I'll call Bob or Mary," Nick continued. "You could go by my house and pick up Gary's book and my manuscript. They are both on my desk in the study. Actually I'd like you to read and compare hem. You'll see there's not much difference between them, except names. That way you'll get to know everything, and draw your own conclusions. Would you mind doing that for me?"

"That's cool," Alana nodded her consent. In fact, the idea appealed to her. She had already heard about Gary Edwards and his famous book on TV, but she had never had the chance to read it. Truth to tell she wasn't really a big reader of books – flipping through magazines was more her style. Instead of sitting down with books, on her days off she preferred going to movies with her friends or to the bar with Tom.

However, she'd make an exception in this case because this situation was special. Alana couldn't very well let Nick down. Besides, she had to read the book and manuscript not just for his sake, but for herself as well. Her interest in his life and curiosity about everything related to him, stemmed from her unconscious attraction to this older mysterious man.

The next morning Alana was off work and pedaled over to Twins South. It wasn't so far from the downtown high-rise building *River Valley* where she resided. Two hours later she returned home, pulled the book and manuscript out of her daypack and lay on her bed to read.

Luckily, Tom was tied up at work for the next couple of days, freeing her to concentrate on the new material before her.

It wasn't an easy read. Although Alana was a smart girl, she was used to reading much simpler stories. She found Nick's thinking unusual and deeply psychological and she couldn't grasp why his book had been stolen – or even why it was so successful. She wondered what its value was. It took her some time to figure Nick out, to penetrate his feelings and discover his personality.

Beyond the simple things, he saw and felt something extra; the explosion of feelings which he poured onto the pages was both amazing and overwhelming, both striking and shocking. Ordinary events were converted into tragedy. They tickled her nerves like a thriller.

At first, Alana read the book only because Nick had asked her to, but then she became fascinated and sank deeper and deeper into its aura. Toward the end, she found she couldn't stop reading it, even though her eyes often filled with tears.

Nick's manuscript was where Alana had begun. Then she read Gary's novel, surprised by his supreme skill in altering names and appearances of the same characters. She had no idea that a professional editor was involved in helping Gary with the changes.

The book was definitely a one-of-a-kind, which made it all the more valuable on the market.

Of course, Nick never had that in mind while he was writing therapeutically, but Gary had grasped its value as he began going through it chapter by chapter. When the idea of stealing it entered Gary's mind, he felt a bit ashamed for a few days. After all, Nick was his best friend. However, Gary was able to overcome his conscience and concluded that there was no 'dirty money' and so engaged an editor to work with him.

Late on the second day Alana was reading the manuscript and book, her mother, Maria, peered into her room.

"Are you going out with Tom tonight?" she asked.

Alana shook her head.

"No, he's working."

"Then, I suggest you take a break for awhile. Let's have dinner together. It's already six o'clock. By the way, what are you reading so intently?"

Alana came to the dining table and showed her the book. "It's Gary Edwards. *My Obsessive Passion.* Have you heard about it?"

"Oh, yeah," Maria replied. "It was pretty popular last year, if I remember correctly."

"And have you read it?"

"Yes. It was one of the first novels I read in English. I must tell you it was pretty difficult for me. I had to look up so many new words in the dictionary. But I finally finished it," she smiled triumphantly.

"Why didn't you tell me about it, Mom?"

"I was sure you wouldn't want to read it. It's really too tragic for you. I think young people don't like that kind of story. This book drenches your soul with compassion and suffering; young people prefer something light and fun."

"Do you know, Mom, that this book was stolen?"

"There was something about that on TV last year, but I thought it was just a way of promoting the sales. They do that kind of actions sometimes. I, in fact, don't believe things like that."

"But the real author was driven to try suicide. He is in St. Boniface right now. I watch him every day."

"Really?" Maria looked at her daughter suspiciously. "So, that's why you are reading it. Is he a young man?"

"Thirty-five."

"He is young," Maria concluded. "Seniors seldom try to kill themselves. They are naturally closer to the end of their life and that forces them to value what time they had left. I am starting to understand them already," she laughed good-humoredly.

She had had Alana at the age of forty and, although she had already turned sixty-two, she didn't look her age. Few people would pick Maria out as a German woman. She was petite and slender, with bright blue eyes and short blonde hair. Her natural hair color was dark-brown but it was graying so she dyed it very blonde. It worked to keep her looking twenty years younger.

Her face was fresh and tanned from all her work outdoors. It was generally wrinkle-free, except a little under her eyes. She jokingly referred to herself as an 'old woman' since Alana had started grade one. It was the first time when Maria had noticed that most of the other schoolchildren's parents were much younger than she was.

However, she didn't take her age seriously and had no problem with it. When people saw Maria with her daughter they assumed she had become a mother in her twenties - so Alana's presence helped her look and feel younger.

"It's a sad story," Maria commented about the book. "It's obvious that the author is a remarkable person."

"Yes. He's quite unusual," Alana smiled. "And very special," she added.

"Oh-oh!" Maria teased her. "Be careful, sweetie. Don't fall in love. It would break poor Tom's heart."

"Don't worry, Mom. Tom will keep pretending to be the son you never had and help you in the building."

"I'm not thinking about me," Maria retorted. "But it's true – I really need a helper. Albert hasn't been feeling well the last few weeks. I don't even know what to do with him. He is very sick. Tomorrow he promises to see the doctor, finally."

"Really? I saw Uncle Albert a few weeks ago. He seemed all right then."

"I know. It happened suddenly. Times are changing. He is already seventy-two. We are all getting older. Yesterday it almost killed me to plant the petunias alone. There were two-hundred-and-fifty of them."

"So many?" Alana questioned. "Why didn't you ask me to help? Mo-om! Don't make me feel guilty!"

"Come on! You are working hard enough," Maria explained. "You need some rest, too. Besides, I thought you looked cute reading so seriously. I glanced into your room and decided not to bother you. So I did three flowerbeds, four vases in front of the main entrance, and all the hanging pots under the canopy. It was a lot of work, sure, but now I am happy. They will be lovely this year: burgundy, yellow and deep pink. It will be a fountain of color!"

"Everybody will know that their caretaker is a real artist!" Alana playfully teased her mom whose favorite thing to do was painting pictures. In fact, their living room walls were full of her creations.

"The residents in the building already know that," Maria reminded her with a smile. Then she grabbed the TV Guide. "Let's watch something together."

She scanned through the magazine, tracing the lines with her finger. Alana collected the dirty dishes from the table and loaded the dishwasher.

"Oh, look at this!" Maria exclaimed suddenly. "There is *Two Evenings with Gary Edwards* on *The Georgia Show* this week. Do you want to watch them?"

"Really? When?" Alana turned the dishwasher on then returned to the living room. She took the magazine from her mother and zeroed in on the schedule. "Oh no! It has just finished. How did we manage to miss that? Actually, I would be interested to see Gary Edwards myself."

"I saw him myself a few times on TV," Maria reported. "He's popular and on a lot of shows. Quite stylish, tall and good-looking man, but also arrogant and haughty! Well, he knows his value, like most geniuses..."

"Mom, he's not a genius! He's just a thief!" Alana insisted heatedly. "You have to know that. He is about the meanest bastard in the whole world! You have to see Nick Bell to understand what Gary has done to his best friend. He is nothing more than a villain!"

"Okay, okay," Maria put up her hands to calm her daughter's growing anger. "Don't take it to heart, sweetie. If you take every suicide case you see in the hospital this way, you won't be able to continue. Security workers, police, paramedics, and all emergency workers need, first of all, to protect their own nervous systems. If they don't, they'll end up with a heart attack from witnessing other people's tragedies. Surely, you know that. You were trained to understand something so basic. Remember that and get your body and mind to relax."

"You're right, Mom. When is the next part of the show on?" Alana asked, looking impatiently through the Guide. "Oh, here it is. On

Saturday. At 6 P.M. Okay, would you remind me, Mom? We have to see it for sure. Now, I'd better go and read some more. I have to finish the book by tomorrow."

"Does your shift start at noon again?"

"Yes. But, please, don't wake me in the morning. I might have to read through the night."

"Okay, if that's what you want."

Maria shook her head, displeased. She had never seen her daughter so wrapped up in the problems of a stranger before and that worried her. The story about the two writers and their book was in the world of high society – not their world. She didn't want Alana to get involved but it looked like she was too late to prevent it.

The next day, when Alana appeared on the third floor at St. Boniface, door 301 was wide open and two men in overalls were painting the walls white. Otherwise the room was empty.

Mystified, Alana inquired, "Where is the patient?" Rooms were usually only renovated after someone died in them.

"You'd better ask the nurse," one of the workers suggested. "They moved him somewhere because of the disaster."

"What disaster?" She had to find out.

Alana ran to the nurse's station but no one was there at the moment. So she called the Security Office by walkie-talkie.

"Where is my patient from 301?" she asked the supervisor.

"He's on the fourth floor, number 415. Jim is with him," was the answer.

Room 415 was quiet when she arrived. Nick was sleeping with IV in his arm. Jim was beside his bed, reading a sports magazine.

"Hi, Jim," Alana whispered. "Why was Mr. Bell moved? And why is he on IV again? The nurse took it away the last time I saw him."

"Oh, Alana," Jim murmured and looked askance at Nick. "You can't even imagine what happened here yesterday! He was like crazy again! I was lucky he didn't kill me."

"Why? What happened?"

"I don't know. I only turned on the TV. I was getting bored just sitting with him hour after hour. I mean, what can I possibly talk to him about? He is so dull. We needed some entertainment so I turned on the TV to *The Georgia Show.*"

"*Two Evenings with Gary Edwards!*" Alana exclaimed. "Oh, shit! Nothing would have upset him more."

"Yeah. I thought it wasn't very interesting so I offered to change the channel. Although he started getting tense and angry watching it, he wouldn't let me find something better to watch. In fact he was very involved and narrowed his eyes while clenching his fists. Then, after one of Mr. Edwards' answers, he completely erupted in violence. He grabbed a glass with ice from the side table and threw it at the TV.

"Well, that was one explosion, I can tell you. Fire, stinky smoke! The screen was blown into smithereens! They bombarded the walls and ceiling. Hell, there was foam everywhere. You know, like pieces of white cotton glued all over me. Man, was it ever hard to get them off my uniform! I even had to brush that damn foam out of my hair."

"Were you hurt?" Alana asked Jim.

"Fortunately, I instinctually covered my face with my hands a second before the explosion. Otherwise, I could have lost both my eyes from the shrapnel. Just look at my hands! Millions of glass chips came through the air and grazed my hands."

Jim stretched out his arms and showed Alana the backs of his hands, now scarred as if attacked by a clawing cat.

"Jesus! It's terrible!" She shook her head in disbelief.

Alana approached Nick's bedside and studied his face intently. She noticed that his face was also full of small scratches. His hands were again bandaged and secured to the handrails of the bed.

"It looks like he's in jail," she observed sadly.

"Of course! He is dangerous!" Jim exclaimed. "Who can be sure that his next outburst won't kill someone? He's mentally ill, I tell you. Nothing more. His problem is he had too much money."

"Well, Jim. It's time for you to go home," Alana reminded him. "I've already signed you out in the office. Have a nice day."

Finally left alone with Nick, she sat near him and stroked his hair slowly and tenderly. Now that she read both the manuscript and the book she felt she understood Nick - his soul was really too pure and too honest to be in this world; to be in the business.

When Nick's father came for visits, Alana could see that the elder Bell was not pleased with his son. It was clear that Nick's irrational behavior was disturbing him. He needed a strong and reliable partner in business, and anyone attempting suicide certainly was a poor choice. Gustav had never expected his son to act this way and he felt totally let down.

What did Nick's future hold now?

Before her days off, Alana said goodbye to a happier, recovering Nick. His nerves had seemed stable. He was calm and friendly with her and the doctor had promised a quick discharge. Suddenly, this damn TV show had set back all that progress and now no one trusted him.

The doctor had placed Nick on medication again. Of course, he should get better soon, but no one was willing to guarantee that he wouldn't turn violent or depressed when released from the hospital. He could run into Gary somewhere or see him on TV again. How could he carry on with so much unhealed pain still inside?

Nick would need a lot of psychotherapy and help. He would need lots of loving support from a good friend who could fill the emptiness in his heart – the void left by betrayal.

Alana leaned over Nick and kissed his forehead as fondly as a mother would her child.

"Don't worry," she whispered her promise. "I'll take care of you. I'll help you. I don't know yet how I'll do it. But I'll be your friend, a true friend. I'll find a way to free you from Gary's curse. I swear."

She gazed at the sleeping face. Her fingers traced his eyebrows, nose and lips. She petted his temple, cheeks and chin. It occurred to her how strange it was that she knew him better now from the inside of his heart than from outside. In fact, she had never touched him before. Alana realized how much she craved physical contact with Nick. She was completely sure he would like her affectionate longings, but while he was asleep, she had her chance to act.

She fondled his hands, finger by finger and inspected each fingernail. She had heard that it was possible to discover a person's character by their fingernails. Alana laughed to herself. His character! She already knew his character better than anybody. No one else had read both his manuscript and Gary's book as attentively as she had. No one else took all his words so closely to heart.

The only thing Alana didn't know about Nick was his body. Now she tried to make up for that. She opened up his blue hospital robe and gazed on his broad chest. With little hesitation she placed her head on it and listened to the steady rhythm of his heartbeat. She was amazed by the warmth of his slumbering body now so close to her.

Gaining in confidence and lost in her feelings, she reached up and placed her hands on his shoulders and lay there in a one-sided embrace for some time. Then he shifted his body. Alana jerked quickly and sat up.

"Excuse me!" she hastily muttered, a little embarrassed.

"No, excuse me, dear," Nick replied, semi-consciously. "I can't hug you back. It seems they've tied me up. I'm not a patient anymore. Instead I'm a prisoner. Isn't it ironic?" he continued bitterly. "We live in a free country where thieves are rich and popular on TV and their victims are treated like dangerous villains."

"Oh, no, please," Alana pleaded. "Don't take it that way. They were just taking care of you and didn't want you to hurt yourself or somebody else. I'll untie you right away. Just promise to be quiet. Do that for me please. Okay?"

Nick nodded.

"Thank you my dear," he said sadly. "I appreciate this."

She unwound the restrains and they both relaxed a little more.

"Did you read my book?" he asked eagerly.

"Yes, I did," Alana gave him a big smile. "Wasn't it clear why I tried to hug you?"

"Did you like the book?"

"Well, I'm not an expert or anything. But I think it's truly amazing. It is certainly tragic and sad. But all these words are nothing compared to the most important thing – I really know you now. I can understand you. I found the answer to my question – why did you do it? I'll help you. I want to do something for you. You'll see. It will be a surprise, but a nice surprise this time. I promise."

Alana leaned over and whispered conspiratorially in Nick's ear, "I have a plan. You have to be patient just one more time for me. I want you to watch Gary on TV next Saturday at six o'clock. He will be on *The Georgia Show* again. I'll get a ticket and attend. But you have to promise me you won't smash up the TV this time. Just grit your teeth tightly and watch. Don't look at Gary – look at me instead. Okay?"

"Talk to the doctor," Nick replied bitterly. "If they tie me up again and give me lots of drugs, I may be able to stand it. Only for your sake. Are you sure you want to do it?"

"Yes, I am. I need it… and you need it, too. It will be the best treatment! Could I have the phone number of your psychologist?"

Nick shrugged his shoulders, thinking maybe she was as crazy as they thought he was.

For the next three days, Alana was preparing her surprise every morning before she began work. She met with Nick's psychologist to discuss the striking treatment she was proposing. She asked him to debate the idea of the shocking therapy with the medical doctor treating Nick at the hospital. They needed to get his permission for Nick to watch the next *The Georgia Show*. She also went by the TV Station and got her ticket to the show.

During her work shifts, Alana talked to Nick a lot and their friendship and trust blossomed. She now regularly hugged him and kissed his cheek in greeting and saying goodbye. He often smiled at this and once gave her a peck on the cheek in return. Alana still refused to admit to herself that she was in love with him. She believed she was just excited about her idea to help him with something extremely important.

Alana had absolutely no time to see her friends, or even Tom. Luckily he was fulfilling his Army reserve service duty for two weeks. His unit had been called up to ship out overseas.

Alana's life was shifting dramatically. She hardly noticed that Nick and his problems were taking center stage in her life now and she had lost all objectivity. She had made herself part of his story.

On Saturday, Alana arrived at the TV Station almost an hour early and chose a spot in the front row. The auditorium wasn't very big. It had only ten rows of plush seats for the audience, which descended toward the stage. There was a semi-circled line of large leather armchairs positioned in the middle flooded in spotlights and surrounded by cameras. They were waiting for Georgia, the popular host of the show, and her guest of the day, Gary Edwards.

Alana felt tense with anticipation, but tried to calm herself down and concentrate on her plan. She had dressed like a modest, ordinary teenager in blue jeans, a blue T-shirt and sneakers. Her hair was done up in a single braid to complete the image she wanted to project. Gary Edwards' book lay on her knees. Her fingers nervously gripped the golden cover, betraying her emotional state.

Alana's professional eye could easily spot a few undercover security guards among the public.

Hello, colleagues, she thought, smiling at them and feeling relieved. It is so nice to see you.

When Georgia appeared to enthusiastic applause, Alana was surprised that she looked much older in person than on TV - she wore very heavy make up what wasn't usually visible on screen. After some opening chat, Georgia introduced Gary Edwards and the audience stood up and cheered. Alana did, too.

Gary bounded in briskly. He was tall, slim dark-haired man; anyone would call him good-looking. Alana wished he were terribly ugly, but he was attractive and rather elegant in his carriage. There was nothing physical she could fault him on, except maybe his insincere smile and arrogant manners. He sprawled casually in his brown armchair, crossed his legs, and smugly answered Georgia's questions as if she were the only person in the studio worthy of his trouble. All the while Alana's eyes were glued to him as she tried to penetrate his mind.

Since this was a follow-up show, Georgia moved into new territory in her interview. She tried to tease out what had occurred in the last few years of his life. The more they talked, the more Alana understood what was wrong with Gary. His voice had a malevolent edge and his eyes were as furtive as a crook.

"We've heard quite a bit about that major lawsuit you had some time ago," Georgia said. "Was someone claiming to be the author of your book? Could you share some details of that story with us?"

God, help him to be strong, Alana thought, imaging Nick watching this. Please, help him.

Gary laughed.

"You know," he started slowly, stretching the words out. "Things like that happen sometimes when you become famous. People get jealous and want to muscle in on your glory. Everyone pretends to be your friend, your neighbor, or even your unsung co-author! Suddenly I've learned of twenty nephews I have who I never heard before. They all want a share of my money, of course!"

A burst of laughter came from the sympathetic audience.

"Did you actually know the person who claimed to have authored your book, or was he just someone off the street?"

Gary smiled shamelessly.

"Yeah, he was someone I used to know. I don't want to give any names. People like him don't deserve the publicity. You know, I'm a kind-hearted and generous man and I certainly don't want to expose him as a thief."

"I'm curious. Did he provide any kind of evidence that he had written the book first?"

Gary's wide grin now turned into a smirk.

"I really didn't pay attention to those details. My lawyer handled everything."

Be patient, my darling, Alana whispered the silent message to Nick. She already regretted suggesting that he torturously view the show. At the moment, she believed that her idea wasn't thought out enough. She had also underrated Gary's meanness and ability to lie.

Hopefully, they had tied Nick to his bed and were ready to restrain him, she thought. Forgive me, my love. I promise you'll get your revenge this evening.

Georgia's interview ended and Gary began taking questions from the audience.

"Mr. Edwards, I read your book and I couldn't put it down. Tell me, was the story of Nora and the cat a pure fiction or did you really know a woman like that? Someone who served as prototype for Nora's character?"

"I knew such a woman," Gary lightened up and playfully explained. "While writing the book, I asked her where she had gotten the idea to use a cat for her pleasure. She assured me it was a real event, something she'd heard from a friend who was a nurse. They had brought a woman to the hospital in really horrible condition – her private parts were shredded and blood was streaming like a fountain. Luckily she had emergency surgery and her life was saved. That woman decided to use the cat's addiction to the valerian tincture for her own sexual pleasure. She had never imagined how crazy the cat would become during their 'session' together. It had become completely mad and tore at her genitals with its claws, almost ending the woman's life."

Gary paused dramatically before continuing. "My dear friend, who was the model for Nora, was extremely interested in the story and told me that she would be much cleverer. 'I would clip the cat's claws first,' she confided. And that's what Nora did in the book."

"Now you can see how important it is to learn from other's mistakes," Georgia interjected, to screams of laughter. Alana couldn't see anything funny in the crude joke and was too tense to laugh anyway.

"Mr. Edwards," the next question came, "have you ever been married?"

"No," the celebrity author responded.

"Then, are you gay"?

"Definitely not."

"Well, we heard that you had very close friend during your university years."

Gary giggled; then thought before answering.

What will he say about Nick? Alana wondered, bracing herself for the worst.

However, Gary was surprisingly open.

"Yes," he said, "I was best friends with Mr. Nicolas Bell. We were studying law and business together. But it was just friendship. We both dated girls."

"You did say 'was', didn't you? Are you still friends?" asked Georgia.

"Not really. You could say we went our separate ways. Our lives took different turns and we drifted apart."

"We heard that you lost your job as an attorney with Bell's Legal Firm. Is that so?"

Gary shifted in his seat, "Let me set the record straight for you. I wasn't fired, I resigned. I was working there temporary while I put my book together. After my book hit it big, I didn't need to work anymore."

A man in the back stood up.

"Mr. Edwards, do you plan to write another book soon?"

"Not yet. My next move is to get married. I can tell you all that I'm engaged to a lovely lady."

The audience cheered.

"And who is the luckiest woman in the world? Won't you tell us?" Georgia exclaimed, pretending to be surprised.

"She is Miss Laura Adams, the model who was our Miss Minnesota five years ago."

Loud applause, joined with whistles and catcalls, filled the auditorium as Laura appeared in the doorway and swept onto the stage. She wore a shiny black low-cut mini-dress, demonstrating her long, well-tanned legs and arms. A diamond necklace embraced her neck and a cascade of golden ringlets covered her shoulders. She was gorgeous and inimitable.

Gary stood up as Laura approached him. They embraced and Gary held up her ring finger to show off her diamond to the public.

"Congratulations, you two!" Georgia exclaimed.

The crowd cheered like crazy. Alana had not bargained on seeing Laura at the studio, but there she was, the very woman who had ruined Nick's life. Alana looked at her with hate, anger and jealousy. Gary and Laura were together after finishing Nick off, each in their own way. Now they were happy, beautiful and successful. They could publicly celebrate their triumph. The unfairness of it all almost brought tears to Alana's eyes.

If God exists, she thought as she bit her lip, how could He allow such blatant cruelty of fate?

Her anger, however, gave her courage to act and fed her determination. Alana was confidant that Laura didn't know the book was stolen. She was going to right this wrong.

The audience settled down after appearance of Laura who sat next to Gary in the large armchair. Alana raised her hand to ask the next question.

"Please," Georgia smiled and pointed at her.

"Mr. Edwards," Alana began hesitantly, "how would you feel, if one day you found yourself in your character Rick's shoes? What if you came home one afternoon and found your wife making love with a cat?"

The onlookers held their breath. Those who had read the book couldn't help but wonder about Laura, however, no one dared to openly express their suspicions. No one anticipated that a shy, young lady in the front row would have the nerve to speak so boldly. Georgia opened her mouth to dismiss the question, but Gary gestured that he would take it.

"Honestly speaking, I would have no problem with it," he said facing Alana with an insincere smile. "Of course, I wouldn't take it seriously. I would see it like a prank, only."

The audience relaxed, a little relieved that the slippery moment passed.

"I see you brought my book for me to sign," Gary continued generously, pointing to the object now pressed to her chest. "Come up on the stage and I'll gladly autograph it." He gestured her forward and took out an expensive pen from his suit jacket.

Alana approached Gary. She paused beside him for a moment to let the TV cameras to catch their faces together and then, without warning, she unleashed her personal attack.

"You are a liar, Gary Edwards!" she announced sharply and loudly to the world. "You are mean! You are the thief who stole the book! In fact, you drove the real author to attempt suicide! You are an accomplished villain!"

Almost shouting her last words and blinking back tears, Alana spat in Gary's face. His eyes registered total disbelief and shock, as he dropped his pen and pulled back from her. However, her aim had hit its mark - her saliva covered his left cheek and nose. In her rage, she then ripped several pages from the book and threw them at him with the torn book together.

"Aaah!" wailed the viewers, whose faces, along with Georgia's and Laura's reflected the horror and disgust they felt. Everything had happened so suddenly that the cameraman got it all on film and it was broadcast all across America. They all witnessed Mr. Gary Edwards wiping the spit off his face.

Laura quickly went into her designer bag and withdrew some tissues to wipe Gary's face. Not surprisingly, she was almost crying.

Georgia picked up the torn pages and the book at their feet, opened the cover and read Nick's inscription to Gary. Puzzled, she shook her head, but tried her best to maintain the dignity of her show.

The security guards ran to Alana, grabbed her arms and removed her from the stage. The TV screen blinked and immediately went to a commercial break.

In the hospital, Nick was watching the show. He had been squeezing both handrails of his bed so strongly that his knuckles turned white. At the end, he threw himself back on his pillow and let out a mad nervous laugh.

"Thank you, my little friend!" he exclaimed. "Thank you, my little heroine!"

Nick laughed louder and louder until he broke into hysterical sob. He rolled over onto his stomach, hugged his pillow and wept like a child. Ramesh, who was guarding him, ran to call a nurse. She wanted to give Nick a sedative, but the doctor advised against it and turned the TV off.

"This is a good sign," he said. "Mr. Bell really needs to let it all out. Crying is the best release for him. Let him alone."

The next morning, Nick felt fine and was discharged from the hospital. Alana, who was questioned by the police but later freed, called him and came to pick him up in a taxi.

STOLEN

She was accustomed to seeing Nick in his blue hospital robe in his room. In fact she only knew him as a patient lying in bed and she didn't realize how tall he was. Yet, there he stood, just a bit shorter than Gary Edwards.

Outside the hospital, dressed in blue jeans and sweater, Nick already looked different – much more handsome. He wasn't a sick and weak patient anymore, someone who needed Alana's care, help and love. Instead he was self-confident and independent.

She sensed the difference right away and grew anxious. However, within seconds, her fear and tension subsided because she could see that Nick was happy and impatient to see her. He had a broad smile on his face. Her treatment worked!

"Thank you, my little doctor," Nick said, hugging and kissing her. "You gave me back my life and I'm really thankful. You are the best girl in the world!"

Chapter 4

"I'M SORRY, TOM. SHE JUST LEFT five minutes ago. Someone from work called her. There's some kind of emergency there. She even had no time to call you first. I'll try to find her and have her call you back." Maria was clearly distressed, "Oh gosh, are you leaving? This evening? So soon? What time did you say? Ten o'clock? Okay, she'll call you. I promise." She hung up, feeling upset and unsettled.

Maria hated to lie and lying to Tom was especially difficult because she liked him so much - he was like her own son. And she knew very well where her daughter was.

Alana had called her the evening before, her voice full of joy and excitement.

"Mom," she said, "don't worry about me. I'll be home in the morning."

"Are you with Tom?" Maria asked. "Are you at the bar?"

"No, Mom. I came for dinner at Nick's new house and I'm staying here tonight."

"You're what?!"

"You heard me, Mom. Don't worry, though. Remember, I love you." Alana quickly put the receiver down.

Dear God, thought Maria. He is an older man from another world. I really don't like this! Alana used to be so happy with Tom. What is going on? What could I say if Tom called? Help me, God, please! Don't let him call for Alana. Please!

However, Tom did call a half-an-hour later. Maria reported that Alana had gone out with her girlfriends and wouldn't be home until very late.

Then, this morning Tom called again at seven. Maria said Alana was still asleep. At eleven o'clock Tom was on the line again. Maria was forced to cover for her wayward daughter once more. It was too much, and she was beginning to feel disgusted with both Alana and herself.

Poor boy, she thought. Here he is, leaving for the war in Afghanistan tonight at 10 P.M. Quite naturally, he wants his long-time girlfriend to see him off. But she's off on a new and dangerous romantic whirlwind. It was a dirty shame if Alana didn't return to earth in time to see him.

Maria could realize the whole drama playing out. She knew that Tom was preparing to be in Afghanistan for six month. He was doing it out of duty but also hoped to get supplementary payments that would help finance the wedding and a honeymoon. Alana had told him she dreamt to be married some day at the blue glass St. Peter's Cathedral in Germany - she had heard so much about it from her mother.

Maria didn't exactly approve of Tom going to war to earn more money. She felt that young people thought of war as if it were merely an adventure. They couldn't understand what real war was like. She had always hopped that Tom would never be called to serve in battle. Even though his turn wasn't supposed to come until the following month, something had pushed the date forward. And so he was shipping out tonight.

This news disturbed Maria, but what really led to the growing knot in her stomach was Alana's new love interest. Maria found it almost impossible to figure out. Restlessly, she paced the living room. Then, in order to distract herself from worry or further phone calls, she headed for the building lobby and started to clean the glass of the main door.

She had almost finished when she saw a brand new, shiny red Ford Focus pull into the driveway under the front canopy. Maria knew it didn't belong to any of the building residents so it must be someone's guest coming to visit. She narrowed her eyes to get a better look through the sparklingly clean doors when Alana jumped out of the driver's seat and ran toward her. Maria cautiously opened the door, amazed at what she was seeing.

"Good morning, Mom! Did I surprise you?" Alana enthusiastically danced around her mother, unable to control her emotions. "Did you see it? Do you like it?"

"What are you talking about, Alana?"

"The car, Mom."

"That new red car? Did he give you a ride or loan you his car?" Maria asked in her confusion. She could tell there was no one else in the car.

"No. I drove it myself. That new red is *mine*! Nick bought it for me this morning!"

"What are you talking about?" Maria's heart skipped a beat. Today things were taking a strange turn. "Is it already going so serious with him?" she asked apprehensively.

"Yeah, Mom. I really love him. Nick is so wonderful...and so special."

"I don't know," Maria shook her head. "I've already heard you say the same words about Tom. Sweetie, you are a light-headed butterfly sometimes. Okay, go and park it downstairs and come inside for lunch. We need to talk."

"Actually, we've already had lunch," Alana admitted, "at his hotel – *Astoria.*"

"What?!"

"Don't worry, Mom. I'll park the car and join you in five minutes. But I'm not all hungry."

Maria prepared some coffee, toast and salad and set their small table. Alana came in, washed up and dutifully joined her mother at the table like an obedient child.

"Mo-o-o-om," she begged her mother. "Please don't be upset with me. I know you are pretty old-fashioned and all this might be a little shocking to you. You don't want your daughter sleeping with two different men, but I assure you it's actually nothing compared to most of my friends. You might think I'm frivolous and playing around, but I'm quite serious.

"Yes," she continued, "I thought I was in love with Tom, but now I realize I wasn't, not really. Yes, he's a good special friend. I still like him a lot and he's fun to be with. But love, I'm learning, is something very different. I can't exactly put it into words very well, but I'm dying from love for Nick. I never meant to cheat on Tom, it just happened. Right now I'll tell Tom it's all over between us."

"I'm afraid it's too late," Maria shook her head and looked hard at her daughter. "Tom's leaving for Afghanistan tonight. You must see him off as his loyal girlfriend and not tell him anything different. If you say anything, you'll break his heart and who knows what will happen over there to him? He might do something reckless or be very depressed and you might be responsible for his death. War, you must know, is not just a vacation trip or some kind of joke. It's a matter of life and death."

Maria's voice hushed as she continued, "I was five years old when the war in Europe ended, but I still remember the bombs falling on Berlin. You can't even begin to know what that was like. I still hear them and the old feelings of horror come back to me, from the bullets passing and buildings crashing. You may see things like that on TV or in movies but you never lived in. I definitely don't want Tom to be killed or handicapped because of your fickle heart."

"Then, do you want me to lie to Tom?"

"No. You made *me* lie to him already. He has called three times for you. I couldn't very well tell him you were spending the night with another man. It was none of my business. You and Tom have to sort out yourselves what you want to do about the future. That's why I stayed

44

out of it and just made some excuse for you to buy some time. I didn't appreciate having to lie. But now the situation has changed. Tom is flying out tonight so give him a warm and worry-free send off. It's your duty to keep quiet and let him go away with a peaceful heart. I'm serious, Alana. You won't be lying, you be humane!"

"Okay, Mom," Alana replied. She rarely saw her mother so impassioned and felt a little robbed of her earlier jubilant mood. "I understand. I just don't want you to be against Nick."

"I am not against Nick. Actually, how could I be? I've never met the man. I just know that he is high-society, older than you and divorced. Oh, and he has writing talent, went through suffering and ended up tied to a bed in the hospital. Am I right?"

"Oh, Mom, he's much more than that!"

"Okay. I see that he has a generous heart, since he gave you such a beautiful present. Maybe he is serious about you, too. At least I hope so. But I can see a lot of problems ahead for you if you spend time with him. Do you think for a moment his family would be happy if he were to marry an immigrant caretaker's daughter?"

"You aren't only a caretaker, Mom. You and dad were very educated and talented people - journalists at the largest German newspaper."

"Forget it, sweetie. That was a quarter of century ago in another country a world away from Minneapolis. I came here with no language skills at all and had to wash floors in a bar. Then I moved up a little and was a housekeeper in hotels. What else could I do? I had to support us somehow. Even this simple resident manager position – it took me ten years of living in America to qualify for it. I'm sure you know what it cost me. No, Alana, your level of society matters here. We are far below that man. Even if he does love you, even if he is serious about you, I don't believe any good will come of it."

"I don't know, Mom," Alana sighed sadly. "I wouldn't go that far. I'm not sure that Nick ever wants to marry again. And I'm not sure I'm ready to marry. You know what my goal is and I haven't reached it yet. That comes first with me. You know that, Mom."

"But you've already messed up your chances," her mother protested. "You caused a scandal on that TV show. Then you were questioned by the police. Probably Gary Edwards will try to sue you for some crazy amount of money. All that can't be very good for a career in police work. I'm afraid you're acting too childishly, dear. I can't help but worry. Do you see how much you've changed in the just the last few weeks? I had hoped that you got older you'd become more responsible and mature. But that's not happening and, I'm sorry but I don't know how to help you."

45

Maria finally let all of her frustrations off her chest. Alana pulled her chair closer to her mother and gave her a big reassuring hug.

"You don't have to do anything, Mom, honest. I'm sorry I'm so impulsive sometimes and just lose my head. But you sound like a worried old woman. I think you've forgotten what love is like. Can you even remember what it's like to be crazy in love? I know you loved daddy, but it was so long ago. Have you ever thought about your life here in America? You've always worked so hard to raise me. Uncle Albert and Ant Luisa helped us a lot, of course. I'm so grateful to all of you, but I'm not a child anymore.

"I'm an adult – a grown woman – and you don't need to be a full-time mother now. You need to have your own life. I even think you should find a man friend. I want you to find happiness again. You need to think more about yourself and your future. That will be more productive than to worry about me."

Maria let out a laugh.

"Really, it's true. You are an adult, my dear," she said, warmly hugging Alana. "Sometimes I forget that. But, please, don't make fun of this old lady. How could I possibly find a man and find love when I am over sixty years old? My heart is dead. My soul is dead. Even my aged body is dead. I went through the change five years ago. So I am all finished being a woman. Your mother, I'm afraid, really is an old woman. The only thing I can look forward is being a grandma, if one day you'll bring me a baby.

"But for now, these are my babies," Maria gestured to her paintings on the walls of their living room. "I paint them. I love them. I talk to them and dream about them. They are my happiness and I am absolutely satisfied with that. I don't need a man in my life. In fact all that I need now to feel more complete would be your child."

"You know, many seniors date and even marry each other," Alana objected. "It's very common. You can look in some magazines or newspapers. There are hundreds of personal ads and some agencies."

"Why not?" Maria tried to humor her daughter a little. "They can do it if they want or need to. But I don't need it. I have a good job in a beautiful building; I'm surrounded by nice people. I have my paintings. I also have you and Albert. We're really close with him, especially now that Luisa died. Can't you see that I'm already happy and don't want to go out looking for problems? That's why I'm so concerned that you are starting to bring problems into our life."

"Promise me you won't worry anymore, Mom. I can handle all my problems myself."

"Well, my big girl," Maria said, and kissed Alana's cheek. "You can begin by calling Tom right away. Then I want you to go and see him. Even if you don't want to do it, please, do it for me. For the last time. If you had anything planned with Nick for tonight you must cancel it. Just this once. For Tom's sake."

"Of course I'll call Tom," Alana assured her. "Nick is busy tonight anyway. In fact, for the next few days. He's starting a new life and needs to see his father about the family business. He's missed many things and they have to work out new arrangements. Besides, he has a new house to settle into. His father bought it while he was in the hospital. There was no way he could return to the Twins South place where he tried suicide..."

"Okay, okay. I'm tired of hearing about him right now," Maria put her hands over her ears. "Just go and call Tom."

Alana took the phone, went into her room and shut the door. She stretched out on her bed, rested her head on her pillow and sank into reverie about Nick.

Overflowing with her feelings, she pushed away any guilt she felt toward her mother or Tom. She was proud of how she had spoken up to her mother, trying to help Maria make her own private life that didn't center on Alana.

Lying on her pale green quilt, she wanted to drown in the new and powerful experience of love that her amazing night with Nick had brought.

In fact, it had been a restless night. They had had sex five or six times. Alana couldn't even remember exactly how many. They only slept a little and were aroused again and again by the hot presence of their bodies together. She was actually quite exhausted, but incredibly happy, as well. Her heart and mind was full of Nick. Every cell of her body called out for him. He lips were even swollen from their endless, passionate kisses. She didn't really want to take a shower and wash his touches, his very smell away. She wanted to hold on to it forever.

Nick was so strong, so wild and so hungry, so unlike Tom. Alana understood now the taste of a mature man and felt herself wise, experienced and excited. She sensed bonded with Nick and couldn't live without him for a day.

Her mind refused to think about Tom. If Alana had had any choice in the matter, she wouldn't have even talked to him now. She knew it would be impossible to embrace him sincerely. Or even look into his trusting brown eyes or stroke and muss his short dark-brown hair like she used to do. Her man now must have long, blonde hair and hot green eyes.

Really, she mused, it is fate. Tom was leaving at just the right time.

Alana knew it would be extremely difficult to be with Tom again, today. She would consider it a betrayal of her love for Nick. However, she admitted that her mother was right. It was her duty to see Tom off and give him a friendly farewell for the last time.

She understood it would take all of her effort to be Tom's 'girl' for one more evening, but determined to be strong and charming. Slowly she awoke from her daydream and reluctantly dialed Tom's number.

"I'll pick you up in half-an-hour, honey!" Tom announced happily. "Put on something special. The farewell party at City Hall starts at five. That will give us a couple of hours to cuddle before."

"Let's go straight to the party, then," Alana suggested. "I'm not feeling too well today."

"What's the matter?"

"I've got cramps."

"What again? You had them just two weeks ago, if I remember correctly."

"Yeah, but now I have them again."

"Something must be wrong with you. I think you'd better see your doctor about it."

"I will, Tom. Let's just go to the party tonight. Okay?"

"Anyway, I'll be by in thirty minutes to get you. We can go to the park and smooch on the benches like love-sick teens. I need something to remember you with. I love you, honey."

"Okay," Alana barely whispered her consent. Every fiber of her being was saying, "There is no way I can do it." Then she decided to look at it as part of her 'hero training' and use her sense of humor to help get through.

City Hall was beautifully decorated with red, white and blue flowers and flags for the occasion. The garlands, balloons, enlarged photos of Afghanistan, soldiers' camps, and veterans covered the walls of the ball-room. Candles and red carnations adorned fifty round tables, set up to seat six people apiece. Each mobilized soldier was to have a table and could invite up to five guests. Besides Alana, Tom was surrounded by his folks and his two older sisters, who came from Duluth especially to see him off.

Alana was quite close to Tom's family so they were all very comfortable together.

Tom's good friends sat at other tables, and Alana recognized some of her girlfriends and former classmates. After a wonderful roast beef dinner, they were all shown a short film on the mission ahead and its importance. Then they brought on a local choir to sing, followed by a professional performance of cadets. The early evening climaxed with a dance and fireworks.

Everyone was in a good mood, except for a few mothers dreading sending their young sons so far away. Alana felt right at home with the crowd - this was the life she had been raised with. She was caught up in the energy and elation and had to admit it was good that her mother made her come. The idea briefly crossed her mind that she would like to bring Nick to something like this in the future. Perhaps this was the kind of community he needed to change his gloomy mood and help him adjust to his new life.

Tom called all his friends over to his table.

"Okay, guys," he said and pulled a small jewelry box out of his uniform pocket. "I want you to witness this. Right here and right now I'm asking Alana, this lovely young lady at my side, to marry me right after I return from Afghanistan."

He went down on one knee and took her left hand. Swiftly, before she had time to think about what was happening, he placed a gorgeous ring with three mounted diamonds on her ring finger. Everyone cheered, laughed, and shouted their congratulations. Tom's mother and sisters, as well as Alana's friends rushed to hug and kiss her. Her shock was real enough. It was all quite overwhelming.

Tom's proposal had been so sudden and unexpected that now she felt dizzy and faint from the crush of people around her. The timing was totally wrong. This was the last thing she wanted to happen tonight. Of course, Alana had sensed that Tom might propose to her, but thought it most likely after he came back from duty.

Not now, not this moment, she thought.

She had already given her heart to another man and nothing could change that. With horror, she felt she was astride two ice floes, each one floating away and ripping her apart. She was speechless in her anguish and she couldn't share her heart with anyone around.

The crowd of the well-wishers had temporarily separated the young couple, and given Alana some breathing room. What answer could she possibly give Tom? She had no idea what she could – or would – say.

However, Tom pushed his way back to his beloved's side, put his arm around her waist and invited her onto the dance floor. He was beaming with joy, like a love-struck knight. Alana yielded to his strong guidance as the band struck up a slow, romantic tune. Together they stepped into a dancing circle, and, as Tom's arms encircled her shoulders, she softly rested her head on his collarbone. It was comfortable to cling to each other like this; Tom was stocky and not very tall and they had often danced in this position.

"Are you happy, honey?" Tom asked her now "Will you wait for me?"

Alana nodded, as her eyes filled with tears. A sob stuck in her throat and remain unvoiced. The music was so slow, beautiful and sensual – they were playing this evening the same song that she and Nick had enjoyed together the previous night. Alana could barely suppress her feelings. The tears streamed down her cheeks. Tom responded to all this emotion by pressing her even closer to his heart.

"Thank you, honey," he whispered fondly, kissing her ear and the hair at the back of her neck.

Alana felt that this was the last time she would ever see Tom. She was certain that they would never be together. Why did she sense that? Would he be killed? Would she marry Nick? She couldn't say exactly, but she just knew that they were parting forever. Her tears become a sort of farewell. It was a sad and painful moment.

After taking Tom to the airport, his parents and sisters drove Alana home, considering her already part of their family. It was after eleven. Her building looked and sounded dead. Most of the residents were of working age and already retired for the night because they started their mornings early. Alana was sure her mother would be asleep too.

When she unlocked the apartment door she was surprised to see all the lights on. The smell of paint hit her. There, Maria stood in front of her easel, holding her palette in her left hand and a brush in the other. She was painting, something she usually did when suffering great stress. Then, as Maria turned to greet her, Alana saw her reddened eyes full of tears.

"Mom!" she called out with alarm. "What happened?"

"Albert," Maria answered, chocking with tears. "He was diagnosed with cancer today – a really bad case of cancer. His doctor says he only has a month to live."

"Oh, no!" Alana tried to comfort her mother. "Are you sure? Maybe it's a mistake?"

Maria shook her head and bit her lower lip. Then she placed her weary head on Alana's shoulder.

"I can't live without him," she confessed, sobbing in despair. "He's the last thing left of my life in Germany. I have nothing else. Everything is finished to me."

Chapter 5

A FEW DAYS LATER NICK called Alana at work.

"I have some news for you, baby," he said. "Do you want a laugh? Georgia's assistant called me from *The Georgia Show* and invited us – you and I – to be guests on the next show and tell our story. How's that for a laugh?"

"Why did she do it, do you think?"

"Well, Georgia picked up the book you tore up and threw at Gary. You were so worked up that you missed it, but on TV everyone saw Georgia read my letter to Gary with interest."

"What do you think about it, Nick?" Alana asked worriedly. "Do you want to go?"

"Absolutely not! That chapter of my life is over for me. I'm trying to completely forget about it and I don't want to do anything to stir things up again. Remember that I already endured a year of lawsuits over it and that finished badly. I just wanted to let you know because the media may come looking for you. I didn't say anything about you, but, eventually, they can find you. I really don't want any more involvement in this whole mess. I appreciate that you stuck your neck out for me, but now you don't have to suffer anymore on account of me."

"But you could tell your side of the story to the world. And it might be an interesting experience," Alana tentatively proposed.

"Please, don't even think about it. This morning Georgia herself called my dad to ask him to persuade me to come. She thinks it would be a hit show and create a lot of interest. My father refused, of course. The label 'suicide' is hardly good advertising in the business world. We must keep everything private and not go washing dirty linen in public. I don't need a show like this. And I certainly don't want to deal with it. It's my choice, okay, baby?"

"Well," Alana took a deep breath. "It's up to you, of course. You know, Nick, I miss you so much."

"Me too. Okay, baby. I'll call you in a few days. I'm completely snowed under by my father's huge new project. He wants me to be the executive director of it and it's so time-consuming."

"But surely you have some free time during the evenings. Couldn't we go out to a bar or a dance club?"

"Sorry. It's all too much for me, my dear little friend. You forget that I'm not as young as you are. I long ago left my student days behind. Besides, all that is too connected in my mind with Gary. I definitely don't want to go back. It's better for me to just come home and relax in my tanning bed or in the hot tub."

"Yeah," Alana whispered sadly. "Couldn't we just relax together?"

"Sure, baby. We will. I'll call you later. Okay?"

"Okay. Take care. Don't work too hard."

"I'll try not to," Nick laughed. "Got to run. Kiss you, baby."

There were few outward changes to Alana's life. She continued working her shifts at the hospital, saw her friends, and went out to bars and dances. The major difference was that she started practice driving her new car on her days off, which really made her happy. Every time she touched the car it reminded her of Nick. She could feel that she was with him again.

Alana also began watching business news on TV, hoping to catch some information about Nick, his father, or their company. Every small detail she could pick up about the Bells was important and interesting to her; she was hungry to learn more and more.

At work, Alana began reading *Business Week* instead of the *Enquirer* to get a better idea of how the business world worked. The more she invested, the more love burst her heart open. Sadly though, she had to admit that her give-and-take was with TV shows and magazines, only, and there was no one around her she could share her growling feelings.

She couldn't tell her girlfriends about Nick because they all knew Tom. They were also going out with Tom's friends, so the circle was a tight-knit one. Alana was even forced to lie about her new car to them. She told her friends that she had saved enough money to buy it herself, and she had also gotten it at a great discount. Alana didn't like having to lie... but how else could she hope to protect Tom?

Her mother was seldom home these days, since she spent every free minute at the hospital with her dying brother. During the brief moments they were together, Maria mostly reported on Albert's condition or quickly asked her daughter if she had heard anything from Tom. Alana new Maria had no interest at all in Nick, which really hurt her.

One day, she drove her mother to visit Albert. She came into his room to say good-bye to the only father figure she had ever known.

Albert was lying in bed, pale and weak. He was so close to death that it reminded her of Nick – the first night after his suicide attempt. It was pitiful to see her uncle so fragile and helpless. He had been Alana's strength and guide, as he helped her go through girlhood. She cared deeply for him and knew he loved her very much.

Maybe, she thought, Uncle Albert could be the one person I can share my happiness with.

She hugged him and kissed his colorless cheek.

"Uncle," she whispered directly into his ear. "I want to tell you a secret. I'm in love. I'm really in love. It's not Tom. It's another man."

Albert kissed her cheek in return and fondly petted her hair. Slowly he formed his words and softly spit them out.

"It doesn't matter to me who he is," he said. "It only matters that you are happy. That's all. Life is too difficult without happiness. But I do one request for you, sweetie. If you ever have a son, please name him Albert after me. It would mean so much to me, if my spirit could pass on and stay alive in our family."

"I will. I promise," Alana assured him. Her dying uncle's request seemed like a good idea to her. It even made her happy to be able to give him such a gift.

She was still waiting impatiently to hear from Nick but, instead of him, Tom had called Alana twice. It was very difficult to hold a conversation because of the static on the line from Afghanistan. Alana got the message, anyway, that he was okay and she tried to convey that everything at home was still the status quo.

Nick didn't call her as he'd promised and Alana didn't dare to call him first. She had to suffer in silence.

In a week, Alana got a call from the police officer who was responsible for her case. He reported that all the paperwork was complete and sent to Gary Edwards. It was up to him now, to press charges against her or not.

Alana decided that it gave her a good excuse to finally phone Nick up.

She was a little surprised to catch him at home; he sounded sad and tired.

"Don't worry, baby," Nick responded to her news. "If Gary tries to start something, I'll find you the best lawyer imaginable. Even with a worse case scenario, I'll cover all expenses. So, you have nothing to worry about."

"I'm not really worried, Nick. I'm just missing you... terribly," Alana admitted shyly. She tried to hold back the passionate torrent she actually felt.

"Thank you, my dear little friend. I appreciate it. Sorry, but I had no chance to see you. I've been out of town. My dad took me to Hawaii for a week. I really needed to relax and recuperate. In fact, I just got in a few minutes ago."

"Weren't you well?" Alana asked worriedly. "What's the matter?"

"Honestly speaking, I don't really like what I'm doing." Nick took a deep breath and continued, "Working in business, in truth, brings me down. It reminds me too much of the past - too much of Laura and Gary. I can't live that life anymore. I need to change something in my existence, actually. I'm thinking of moving away. But I don't know yet what I want. I messed things up. Now I need some time to forget the past and sort out the future. My psychologist recommends travel. But I haven't decided yet where or when or how."

"I could go with you!" Alana proposed.

"Thanks for offering, baby," Nick chuckled. "You are so cute. But you have your work, your family and friends here. You couldn't leave all that."

"Yes, I could," Alana objected strongly.

"No, I couldn't accept another sacrifice from you. You already did a lot for me. But don't worry. I'm staying put for now. I'm just sharing some possibilities with you. I'll call you in a few days and, hopefully, see you."

Alana hung up really confused. All the mixed signals she was getting threw her for a loop. He might leave town! Without her! She knew she couldn't live without him. She'd go with him anywhere, anytime! She had chosen to spend her life with him. He was her destiny. That was all there was to it.

After that call Alana shifted her driving practice to Nick's new neighborhood of Greenwoods. The area was expensive, beautiful, quiet and prestigious. Some lovely homes were hidden away in a small stand of woods. Each of them was uniquely designed and set in a manicured landscape with gardens and fountains blended with the local creek and pine trees. It was there that Gustav Bell had chosen a house for Nick while he was in hospital.

It's exactly what Nick needs, Alana thought, seeing his house for the first time. He can come home from work and truly relax in this setting. It's the best place to find peace and solitude. Mr. Bell must be very wise and sensitive to have selected it.

Every evening after work, from now on, Alana was drawn to the place and drove slowly around Nick's house. She would stop for awhile, hoping to catch sight of him, and then drove on. Sometimes she parked and stood behind the bushes and waited for some action. Several days passed but her trips were all in vain. The house looked totally dead.

One evening, as she was sitting in her car beside Nick's house for two hours, Alana saw Bob, the caretaker, appear. He opened the garage door and drove Nick's silver Mercedes out into driveway. Then he grabbed the garden hose and started to wash the car.

The first time Alana had met Bob was when she had come to pick up the book and the manuscript from the house at Twins South. The second time she saw both Bob and Mary as they were serving the dinner at Nick's hose, when she brought Nick home after hospital and then spent the night there.

It might be a good opportunity to talk to him now, Alana believed. At least I can find out something.

She started the car, circled the block and pulled up behind Bob in the driveway.

"Hi, Bob!" she called and waved. "How are you doing?"

He turned, a bit startled, and looked hard at her. He couldn't place her at first.

"Oh, Miss Alana," he said, finally recognizing who she was. "I'm fine, thank you. This is so unexpected. Nobody told me you'd be coming by today."

"Oh, I was just passing. I'm improving my driving skills in the area," Alana laughed to make it sound casual and spontaneous. "By the way…is Nick at home?"

"No, Miss," Bob shook his head. "Mr. Bell picked him up today."

"Okay. Just tell him I said, 'Hi'."

"Will do," Bob nodded.

"Sorry, I can't stay longer," Alana smiled. "I need to keep practicing."

She drove away, feeling clever and almost contented. It was a good idea to remind the love of her life that she was still around. She was even confident that he would be phoning her any day now. But still, no word from him.

It was a week later when Alana was driving in Greenwoods as usual, that she parked her car beside Nick's driveway, behind the tall hydrangea bushes. She waited almost two hours, like a stalker, craving to meet him and it finally happened that she saw him in something other than her dreams.

Nick had driven home from the office, pulled his car into the driveway and got out. As he turned to take his briefcase out of the backseat, Alana jumped out of her car and bounded up to him, breathless. He was caught as she, without warning, threw her arms and excitedly hung on his neck like a child.

"Hi, there!" she exclaimed happily. "How unexpected! I was practicing my driving here and I suddenly saw you!"

Her eyes shone, beseeching his, and she started kissing him impatiently and hungrily. Nick was so taken aback that he couldn't say anything about the love assault on him. He recovered a little and began responding to her passionate kisses. Unconsciously, he wrapped his arms around Alana's waist and was soon caught in the throes of passion himself. They intensely clung to one another for ten minutes, unable to tear themselves away. Finally, Nick picked her up in his arms and swept her into the house.

"I miss you…I want you…" Alana breathily cried out between kisses.

"I want you, too," Nick answered, as they headed straight for the master bedroom. The urgency of their ardor made them rip off their clothes to quickly get to each other's flesh and pleasure spots. It was the same craziness as their first time, and, again, continued through the night. What she had been longing for this past month had finally happened.

Close to morning, Alana realized that she had forgotten to call her mom.

It doesn't matter, she decided sleepily. Anyway, she is with Albert at the hospital…

When Alana finally awoke in the late morning, she found a note on the bedside table. It read: 'Good morning, baby! Sorry, I have to leave today on a business trip. I didn't want to wake you up. Mary will make you some breakfast. I'll be back in three days. See you, Nick.'

However, more than a week went by and Nick still hadn't called her. Frustratingly, even the surveillance of his house brought no results. He simply wasn't there. Alana started to go a little crazy. She couldn't figure out what to do. Where was he? How can she contact him? Maybe his trip had been extended.

She looked up his office phone number in the phone book and dialed. A nice secretary's voice answered, "Mr. Bell is in a meeting and it won't finish for about one hour. Would you like to leave a message?"

"No, thank you," Alana said, feeling totally crushed. "I'll phone later."

She hung up with dejection. Nick was here, in the city! At work. He must have a beautiful secretary. And he hadn't even thought to call her. Why? She was about to cry. What happened? He loved her. He was so amazing in bed. He wanted her – that was for sure. Was he just terribly busy? Was he seeing other woman? Sure as hell not! He was too hungry for her last time. He was passionate and raring to go.

Alana decided that Nick needed and loved her. She should just relax. Everything would be fine when she saw him. He was just a little bit strained…overloaded, tired, too busy, too lonely. Maybe he's even staying with his father temporarily and that's why he isn't coming home.

That's okay, she thought. I'll catch him downtown.

She wrote down the office address and got in her car.

Alana parked in the lot and walked inside the gleaming towers. She even took the elevator to the eighteenth floor to the entrance of *Bell Legal Services* and stood by the door, reading the golden letters. However, she didn't dare peek inside.

Through the door Alana heard that the place was full of bustling noises: voices, phones ringing, laughter. She froze in terror, imaging what would happen if the door suddenly opened and Nick walked out. There was no way she could make it look like an accidental meeting. He would realize that she was watching him and probably be very angry. That was the last thing she wanted.

Alana felt very out-of-place, but still, it was hard to force herself to leave. She desperately wanted to see his smile. Every cell of her body craved his touch, his hands and lips, and wanted to press against him and feel his warmth. She was famished for his love and tenderness and couldn't live without him.

Luckily, nobody exited while she stood rooted to the spot. Finally Alana managed to board the elevator and return to street level.

She noticed a small park across the street and headed for a wooden bench at the corner. There was a sweet rock garden with a little fountain surrounded by vines. A huge elm tree loomed up behind the bench. The light warm summer breeze blew the seeds from the tree and they covered the bench, he rocks, and the flowerbeds and floated in the fountain. Some of the seeds flew into Alana's hair and onto her shoulders but she ignored them.

Alana's anxiety could be read in her posture. Her body and eyes were trained on the tower entrance and the nearby underground parking exit, not knowing which Nick would choose to use. She wasn't even sure if the building had any other exits.

A couple hours passed. As dusk arrived, the sparkling city lights came on. Tiny lamps studded the park walkway and lit the rocks inside the rock garden. They looked like glow-worms or fireflies and added a touch of magic to the urban landscape.

Then Nick appeared so suddenly that, at first, Alana couldn't believe her eyes. A group of twenty professionally-dressed men and women emerged from the restaurant on the main floor. Nick was among them. They paused under the canopy to continue their conversation, laughing all the while. They flirted and teased one another, and Nick joined in. He seemed to be in a very good mood.

Alana eyed them, uneasily.

Wearing a black suit, white shirt and tie, Nick looked more handsome to her than ever. He struck her as more confident and independent, more adult and mature than she had seen him before. He really was the man who deserved her full admiration and worship. Nick was truly the man of her dreams, but he was from a different world and that difference she now sensed more than ever. Alana was the outsider and it made her feel scared and perplexed. However, her affection for him was so dear that she could overcome such obstacles and claim his love.

Some of Nick's companions began lighting cigarettes. She saw him wave goodbye to them and cross the side street to the convenience store. She ran after him.

When Nick disappeared inside the store, Alana took a deep breath, counted to ten and walked in. She slipped, hidden, behind some shelves and observed him. He took some gum and mints from the display and strolled to the cashier. Alana quickly grabbed the same items and sneaked up behind him. She tapped him on the shoulder and said, "Surprise!" laughing. "I just stopped in to get some gum and suddenly saw you. What brings you here?"

Nick grimaced, with a strange expression on his face.

"It's interesting," he noted. "We picked the same gum. It looks like we have the same taste. Don't you think it's strange?"

"We love many of the same things," Alana meaningfully answered, looking into his eyes. "I miss you, Nick. I miss you horribly."

She hugged him and even tried to kiss him.

"Well," he softly pushed her away. "Let's pay for the gum first and go outside. Okay, baby?"

Nick paid for her items as well and then bought a little bouquet of pink tulips for her at the counter.

"Thank you," Alana said, dying from joy.

As soon as they got outside, Alana pulled him over to the park and pushed him down on the bench where she had spent hours waiting for him. Then she plopped down in his lap, threw her arms around him and began plastering his face with wet kisses. At first Nick tried to object, but very soon he lost control and answered her needy lips.

"Not here," she pleaded when he began to unzip her jeans. "Not here, please. Let's go somewhere. To my place! It's very close, just five minutes away. I'll drive. My car is just around the corner."

Alana stood up and took his hand as she scooped up the tulips from the bench. Nick followed her silently, breathing heavily. They drove without a word, their bodies filled with lusting. When she unlocked the door of the apartment, Nick only whispered, "Where's your mother?"

"Don't worry. She won't be home until morning. She's at the hospital. Just wait a minute. I'll turn on the light."

Alana walked into the kitchen in the dark. Nick could hear the water running and realized she was putting the flowers in a vase. Then she entered the long corridor and turned on the reading lamp in her bedroom.

Nick stood beside the front door in the darkness and waited. He could tell that the dining room was in front of him and beyond that was the larger living room. Light from the street oozed in through the lacy curtains and threw fantastic shadows on the walls. He couldn't make anything out very clearly. Yet, for some reason Nick felt something mysterious about being here. The air hung with an unusual smell that Nick couldn't quite identify. Still, it excited him and caused him to tremble a little.

"Come here," he heard Alana's voice from the bedroom. He walked down the hallway mesmerized. When he entered her room, the strange feeling of excitement disappeared.

Alana's room was full of stuffed animals like a child's room. The teddy bears, cats, dogs, tigers and rabbits were sitting on pillows, on the bedside table, on the shelves and even on the floor. They were everywhere. Nick almost chocked with laughter, seeing them all. His desire took a nosedive.

"Don't you think it's blasphemy to have sex in front of all these innocents?" he asked, teasingly.

"Don't you like them?" Alana asked in return, feeling offended. "What's the blasphemy? Do you think I'm just a little girl? Okay, I'll take them away," and she started to shove them from the bed to the floor.

"Stop it," Nick said, squeezing her hand. "Sorry, baby. I didn't mean to hurt you. Forgive me...please. Forget it. I was just a little surprised with them."

Without a word, Alana returned to kissing him and searching out his manly form and in a minute everything was forgotten. Nothing mattered to either of them except the joining of their bodies in passion and release. Their copulation this time continued half the night until they dropped off completely drained.

At four o'clock in the morning, Alana drove Nick back to his office to pick up his car.

"Will you flee again, my pet?" she asked him, begging for some commitment.

"I honestly don't know," he took a deep breath and lowered his eyes before getting out of the car. "I can't say, my dear young lady, for sure. If you could give me some space for awhile it would be great. I really need some time. I need to think and make some decisions. My new life is not going so well. I'll let you know. I promise."

He kissed her on the forehead like a child and gently pushed her shoulders away, as he got out of the car.

Alana drove home slowly through the early morning streets. She felt down. Nick was struggling and she couldn't understand why. She had no way of fathoming his deep emotional currents but could tell she wasn't really a part of the picture. This was torture enough for her so she tried to put all her bad thoughts out of her mind.

Alana was angry with herself. She had already made many mistakes with Nick. Why hadn't she anticipated that he would object to her stuffed animals? Why had she brought him home to show him how poor her family was? And why did she put up with him always calling her 'baby', 'little friend', and 'dear young lady'? It wasn't fair and was humiliating. She wasn't a baby and she definitely wasn't 'little'. She considered herself a full woman and his lover. It seemed to her that he failed to recognize this fact. What had she done wrong? Why? Why? Why? Now his 'beloved question' was uppermost in her mind.

Alana returned home, gathered up all her stuffed animals, put them into a black garbage bag and left them in the garbage room. Then she sprawled on her disheveled bed, and cried into her pillow with despair until she finally dropped off to sleep.

At five o'clock in the morning, Maria arrived back from the hospital. She needed at least three hours of sleep prior to begin her work on the building. Before turning in she made a quick check around the premises, and when she peered into the garbage room she spotted a big bag full of stuffed animals.

"I wonder why they're here," she mused. "I don't know anyone in the building who has kids. Why are they throwing them away? Alana's already grown up but she still likes them a lot. I can't understand. But I can't see them being thrown away like this. I better keep them and try to find a good place to give them as a donation."

She took a big bag, pulled it into the storage room and left in the corner beside the back entrance.

At five o'clock in the morning, Nick was already home, too. He called his office and left a message, saying that he wouldn't be in for a few days. Then he drunk a full glass of whiskey and sunk into oblivion in his king-sized bed. He slept the full day, he next night and half the following day.

Nick woke up feeling worn out and miserable, with a headache. Once again the whole life was disgusting - his soul was hollow, and his body felt the same. His moral backbone had once more deserted him.

Nick rose and took a shower. Then he drunk a glass of water and went out into the fresh air to lie down in the deckchair in his robe under the pines. He was weak with absolutely no appetite and also had no appetite for life at this point. Where was the meaning of his existence? Nick lay motionless and contemplated his future.

The woods were quiet except for a soothing, distant chirp of a songbird. Above him the pine branches quivered on the light breeze and filled his senses with their earthy aroma. He closed his eyes, trying to let go of everything bothering him. Nick filled his lungs with deep intakes of air to still his racing, troubled mind. Why was he feeling so full of gloom and doom today? Could he do anything without messing it up? He should focus on what lay ahead of him.

Nick hated doing business. It constantly pulled him back, reminding him of the years he spent at university with Gary, years working in the law firm with Gary and more so his marriage to Laura. Even though he changed his house and the location of his office, he felt these superficial moves didn't alter anything for him. His lifestyle reminded the same and the same old misery surrounded him.

There was another thing about business, too, unrelated to his past. Nick knew that both business and law were very far from his true heart. They felt unnatural and foreign to him. They were diametrically opposed to what he really wanted to do with his life. Okay, so he now admitted what he didn't want, but that left a void. He couldn't figure out what it was that could really motivate and inspire him.

Nick felt that he needed a change - maybe to leave everything and go away somewhere. But where? Was Minneapolis the problem? He had no answer. Thank God, he reflected, the question was no longer 'Why?'

Nick thought seriously about closing his office, leaving the business and heading for South America to live in the jungle. He had enough money to do it and to live the whole life not working – even three times over. However, he realized, that would only be running away and would most likely be boring and too quiet. He was still young and active, but where could he-should he-put his energy and talents?

Nick's father had placed a lot of hope in him and he feared to let Gustav Bell down. His father had staked his whole life – the business, plans and projects – on his son. While Nick loved and respected the old man and wanted to fulfill his expectations, he still needed a life of his own. What a dilemma: to stab his father's dream in the back or to sell his own happiness down the river!

There was no easy answer, and that was only the first problem he faced.

The second decision he had to make was what to do about Alana. She had been his 'little friend' in the hospital, winning his trust. Then she became his 'little hero' by confronting Gary Edwards. She was brave and honest, not to mention pretty and available. Nick liked her very much. He was also grateful to her for everything she had done on his behalf. She was great, but then…

He might like to date her casually, but he didn't think they'd have sex right away - especially when they just arrived at his new house from the hospital. Nick had wanted to have a lovely dinner together, talk and get to know her a little better, what made her happy and motivated her. In Nick's opinion, sex should only come after a period of time.

Alana had really disappointed him when she jumped on him like a tigress and began seducing him. He yielded to her charms but would never have initiated such intimacy. Maybe Alana noticed that he hadn't been with a woman for a long period and played on that vulnerability. Nick was convinced that she did it on purpose.

In bed she was a child, without experience or sensitivity, just raw lust. He found the affair disappointing, particularly because he had no desire to be her instructor and was bored by the idea of molding this young lady into a mature love mate. Nick was angry at himself, of course, for letting her call the shots in lovemaking. He was just too hungry.

Nick generously bought Alana a car as a gift and felt that that was all. He wanted to close that chapter and never see her again. Everything had been paid off.

Then, the unexpected silly phone call from *The Georgia Show* pushed Nick to call Alana and she began chasing him all over town. He was disgusted by the obsession she seemed to have developed for him and the lengths she would go to in order to trap him. These 'accidental meetings' were so obvious that she must think he was a total idiot to fall for them. Nick's greatest desire was to kick her out of his life, but he was too mannered for that and still too thankful for their revenge on Gary. So he had practiced unresponsive patience instead, hoping she would give up the chase.

Alana had touched the wrong button and naively kept playing the sex card with him. She thought it was 'love'. The more Nick gave in to her entreaties, the more he felt angry with himself and frustrated. His original attraction to her was now dead. He really didn't want to see her again.

Nick discovered that, for all of Alana's youth and childishness, there was a clutching, clawing tigress underneath. He hated that kind of woman, for they possessively held their 'men' in their teeth for their whole life. Nick's character was soft and kind, but at the same time, though, he wouldn't let a woman pressure him into something he didn't want. If she began making demands, he cut her off.

However, Nick couldn't just dump Alana, like he had many girl-friends before. Deep in his heart he still felt he owed her. He had involved her in his life story which made her a bit different from all of his former lovers. Yet she was all connected with what he wanted out of his life: Laura, Gary, the book, the business and the suicide attempt. He decided he had to talk straight to her.

Nick would seriously explain that things were over between them and both of them had to go their own separate ways. He would try to tell her gently, like an older brother, or even a father. She must stop chasing him. They would end as friends and limit their contact to exchanging birthday and Christmas cards and greetings. That was the only way he could deal with her in the future.

After that, he might travel around for a year or a half. Then he would decide what he would do next. This was the resolution that Nick came to after mulling things over reclining under the pines. Now it was time to carry his plan out.

Nick dressed in a cotton checkered shirt and light beige trousers and then dialed St. Boniface's for Alana's schedule. He was told she was working the usual day shift and got off at six. It was already 6:15.

Half an hour would be long enough for her to get home, Nick supposed.

He drove downtown, parked at the visitor's stall at *River Valley* and approached the intercom panel at the main door. He couldn't find 'Miller' anywhere on the list of occupants.

That's strange, he thought. Is this the wrong building?

Nick was quite sure that this was the right building. He remembered it clearly. He just paid any attention to the floor he and Alana had got off the elevator from the underground garage. They had already started kissing and he hadn't noticed at all which button she had pushed. Nick also didn't think about the apartment number. Now he couldn't remember anything that would help him find the right place. He thought for a while and then rang the manager.

"Hello," a female voice answered.

"Hi," Nick said. "I'm looking for Alana Miller, but I can't find her apartment number here."

"Well..." a voice stilled, a little surprised. "Okay," she suggested then, "come on in, please. Alana will be here soon."

Nick opened the mirrored glass door as it buzzed, and stepped into the lobby.

Chapter 6

THE MIRRORED LOBBY WALLS reflected each other and multiplied the four artificial tropical trees in golden pots standing in the corners. Nick felt completely lost in a green mirrored jungle. He struggled to find the right way to go, and chuckled, amused at his situation.

It was funny because he was totally inexperienced with this type of building. He had never visited a residential high-rise before, only office and professional buildings - all his friends and family were home-owners.

Nick slowly searched the lobby looking for the elevator. He finally found it in the back hallway. He realized that the suite he was seeking for must be tucked behind the corner. So he turned right and stopped.

A petite, slender woman stood leaning against the door frame, next to the open door. She had very short blonde hair and looked youthful. At second glance, however, Nick noticed that she was much older; maybe even over forty.

The woman was barefooted, dressed in jeans and a long, stretched black top, all spattered with paint. She stood silently and stared at him, a sad smile playing at the corners of her mouth.

Nick sensed something mysterious about her look. Her eyes had unusual, elliptical shape but were fuller than Asiatic eyes. He found them enchanting and alluring and held his gaze longer than is polite on first meeting. He just couldn't tear himself away and didn't allow her to avert her gaze, either. It's hard to say how long they held this unexpected pose.

Then Nick noticed the strange smell again, which now wafted out through the open door. It had grabbed his senses and spirit the night he had visited the apartment with Alana. It was now clear that it was a paint smell, and triggered something in him that made him feel dizzy. Nick let himself sink into its ether and was transported beyond thought and speech.

"Did you come to see Alana?" the waiting woman finally asked.

Nick could only nod.

"I'm her mother. You can come in and wait. She'll be here any minute."

64

He didn't really hear her words, because he was entranced by her voice. She had a charming accent, with stronger 'r' and a softer 'l' sound. Anyone could tell right away she was a foreigner. Nick really liked it and experienced it as an unforeseen discovery, like finding a raisin hidden deep inside a muffin.

Meeting foreigners had been different for Nick. Immigrants were never on his radar screen and far away from the social circles he inhabited. He had only heard foreign partners discussing business in accented English. Their language skills were usually very poor, but everyone tolerated the situation because there was money to be made.

"Come in, please," the woman repeated, noticing that Nick was standing, filled with uncertainty. She moved aside and ushered him in.

Nick went straight through the kitchen and dining room into the living room. The woman followed him, but only as far as the refrigerator.

"Do you want something to drink?" she asked. Nick mumbled that he did, but his attention was already on the new world opening before him.

That's what I saw here that night, he thought. There were more than shadows on the walls... there were extraordinary pictures.

All the walls were decorated with original paintings. Most of them were large and quite unique. They overflowed with fountains of color and sometimes - objects. Nick was amazed at the impression they made on him.

One image, still unfinished, stood on the easel. The palette on the floor, under the easel, contained fresh paint in blobs and two small brushes next to it. Alana's mother had obviously been painting when he interrupted her. The half-done canvas looked something like a tornado: black and gray were swirled and twisted together. Palm-sized pieces of glass intertwined between waves with raindrops, resembling tears, leaked onto the glazed surfaces.

Nick studied the painting, mesmerized. The tragedy of it all seized and squeezed his throat. He recognized very well what it represented – the end of life.

The woman approached him with a full glass in her hand. She stood silently beside Nick and they jointly gazed at the picture.

"What is it?" he said softly, indicating the painting.

"It's about my brother."

"Is he dead?"

"Almost. You interpreted it correctly. He has cancer. I spent about three weeks visiting him in the hospital. Today I'm not allowed to see him because the doctor is performing a last-chance surgery on him. I'll see him tomorrow."

Nick turned to her and looked straight into her eyes again. She was beautiful – naturally appealing. Not artificially beautiful, like Laura or some models were, but real and alive. It was noticeable that she was older than him but he paid little attention to that. Her good looks overwhelmed him like the beauty of a bright, multicolored forest in the fall. It had a refined quality compared to the beauty of the fresh forest in springtime, which he was more familiar with. It was more polished and plaintive. He wondered if her life experience and past suffering had produced such a special face and filled her eyes with the mystery of existence, which only she was privileged to know.

"What's that?" Nick asked glancing at the glass she had brought for him.

"Cranberry juice."

"It looks strange," he noticed, seeing the pink opal drink. "Where did you get it?"

"I made it myself. I usually pick cranberries in the river valley every September."

"Really? Why not just buy your juice?"

She shrugged. "It's different, as you can see...and will taste differently. It's natural. Actually it costs less, only the sugar..."

Nick smiled reassuringly. He didn't take the glass from her but, instead, put his hand over hers and squeezed her fingers around the glass. "Okay, I'll try it," he said, moving the drink to his lips along with her hand, "but if you poison me, it'll be your responsibility."

"Do I look so wicked?" she laughed at the absurdity of it all.

Nick took a little sip of juice, still touching her hand. The drink was astringently sweet and had an imperceptible aroma of wild bushes.

"Oh, it's nice," he remarked, finishing the glass to the last drop and forcing her to raise her arm, too. "Thank you. It's amazing," he finally released her hand. "I'm going to come here every day to have some."

She eyed him suspiciously. His behavior seemed strange, but she was sure that he was only teasing. She pursed her lips and returned the glass to the kitchen in silence.

"I'm sorry, I didn't introduce myself," Nick said at her back, still smiling and following her with his eyes. "My name is Nick, and you are...?"

"Maria," she answered, rinsing the glass.

"Nice to meet you, Maria."

"Nice to meet you, too," she responded, returning to the living room and looking askance at the wall clock.

When will my naughty girl get home? Maria thought. I'm already tired of him. But for her sake I should entertain him and keep him here until she arrives. Oh, Alana! You were crying so much over him this past month and now he is here. But you aren't. How unlucky can you be?

Nick turned to the paintings again. "I really like them," he said. "Do you paint every day?"

"No. Only when something happens."

"So they must have some special meanings for you," he conjectured.

"Maybe," she shrugged. "Mostly they're my memories of Germany. Each picture represents one point of stress in my life – one time when my soul was paralyzed. I don't know...I needed something to relax. Painting is my only outlet, a way to channel the sorrows of my heart. You should be able to understand that. You have used writing for the same purpose. I can't write and nobody here needs my German. My English, as you can tell, is horrible."

"It's not so bad," Nick objected.

"Oh, I can talk, all right. But writing in English is too difficult for me. So I discovered this way... with painting, somehow...by intuition."

"Your paintings are full of feeling. They're disturbing," Nick noted thoughtfully. "I've never seen anything like them. Maybe in Europe...in some art museums. This long black tunnel, for instance. I can even hear the echo buzzing there. Can you explain it to me?"

Maria glanced at the clock again. It was now 7:15. Where was her daughter?

"Well..." she took a deep breath and replied with reluctance, "it was scary, really scary. There was an echo. I'm happy you can sense it. And I'm proud that I can somehow portray it. I'll tell you the story if you really want to hear it."

She looked at him for confirmation.

"Yes, I do. Sincerely," Nick said imploring her. "It's really interesting and I want to understand more. There's a hidden message I'm eager to uncover."

He sat on the lemon-and-olive colored couch across from the painting, but didn't take his eyes off it.

...The metal lid of the manhole cover closed above them and Klaus turned on his flashlight.

It's like a grave, Maria thought, shivering in her T-slacks and light sweater. In fact it is scary, but I have no choice. Freedom or death!

The dunk, dark tunnel snaked ahead, smelling of rust, earth and something rotten. It was filled with pipes and the water passing through them gurgled and made strange noises. Sometimes they hissed and Maria was startled each time.

"Don't worry. It's only water," Klaus sought to quietly reassure her.

They couldn't speak louder because the tunnel produced a reverberating echo with every sound. It buzzed around them and rolled ahead. Everything made Maria think of hell from the thriller. Klaus, himself, could be the devil, dressed in a black hooded sweater. The flashlight gleam distorted his face with weird shadows. Maria only had the courage to accompany him on this underground trip because she knew him quite well.

Klaus went first, showing her the way. It was visible that he was confident of his steps and had been this way many times before.

"We are pretty safe here," he guaranteed. "Just don't stumble over something. And don't twist your ankle. That's the only real danger."

"Are you sure?"

"Absolutely. Albert came this way a year ago."

He was convincing and Maria put her full trust in him. She knew that Klaus was professional, transporting refugees from East to West Berlin through the underground.

"It's a bit more difficult now, than it was for Albert," Klaus continued. "They blocked the entrance from the tunnel in West Park. They also blocked the tunnel in the middle. So we'll go to the U-Bahn Depot..."

(There Maria interrupted her monologue to explain Nick that that was the German name of subway. Nick was easily drawn out of himself and into her story.)

"...Our people are waiting for us there," Klaus went on. "There is a higher risk of danger at the border, when soldiers are searching the carriages, but believe me, it'll be okay. They increase their vigilance, but we increase our creativity."

"Your also increase your prices," Maria commented sarcastically. All her savings, Peter's car and all her jewelry were sold to finance their escape. She had nothing left but the closes she had on her back. Now her only treasure was her life and Peter's picture in her sweater pocket.

Klaus grimaced, "We are protecting ourselves. You will live in the free West but we, smugglers, will stay here..."

"I know," Maria answered sadly. "I'm just teasing you. I understand everything."

They walked the tunnel for an hour until they located the exit to the U-Bahn Depot through another hatch. There, Klaus handed Maria over to an older, short man in dark blue overalls who was waiting for them beside the open lid. It was Willy, the carriage technician. It spite of his aged appearance, he was lively and forced Maria to hasten to keep up with him as they ran along the length of the train. When they came to the selected carriage, he packed Maria tightly into a black metal box which hung on the undercarriage.

The box was small and Maria found she had to ball herself up, pull her knees to her chin and lay very quietly. Luckily she was petite and limber, otherwise it would be impossible. Narrow cracks near the lid allowed her some fresh air to breathe.

"Your way isn't to long," Willy consoled her, screwing the lid of the box above her head, "just a fifteen-minute ride, a half-an-hour search, and then twenty minutes to the very end of the line. At the West Depot, someone will knock on the wall of the box and say his name is Dittmer. You should answer. Don't sleep. Otherwise, he won't open the box and you'll return back to us.

"You should know that the most difficult part will be when they search at the border. It's right in the middle of your trip. The border guards will put their bayonets inside the box, exactly into the slits you use for breathing. Hold your head carefully to one side and you won't get caught. And, whatever you do, don't make a sound: no breathing, no coughing, no sneezing, nothing! If they hear anything they'll shot you on the spot. It is regulations. It's their duty.

"Oh, and one more important thing – don't get confused in the darkness. You only answer to Dittmer at the end, but not to the guards at the border. They will knock on your box, too. Be really careful about that. Any mistake will cost you your life."

He doesn't need to repeat his warnings, Maria thought, irritably.

She felt she was buried alive in the little, metal casket. Maria sensed she wasn't going to make it but she had agreed to try, being too tired of constant fear and filled with despair. Inside the cramped quarters she closed her eyes and thought back to her parting with Peter.

"Forgive me, my love," she whispered. "Forgive me for everything. I don't know what for, just forgive me, please. I hope your escape will be easier. See you tomorrow…"

Maria broke in the middle of her story. There was a spasm in her throat that prevented her from saying more.

"Did you get past the border? What happen next?" Nick eagerly asked, staring at her with admiration. "Were you successful?"

She just nodded her head and coughed a bit, trying to get a grip on her emotions.

"You see, I am alive today. I have another painting from that experience," Maria pointed at a canvas that was illuminated with a miraculous blue light, with a burst of azure, silver and white. It rang with new found life in the sunshine. Like a wellspring of rebirth, it told of delirious happiness.

"Tell me about it, please," Nick asked. "It might be what I really need."

...Maria answered Dittmer's knock on the box, but by the time he had removed the box from the train, she had passed out. She was paralyzed and looked like a corpse; the tension of her dangerous journey had put her in shock.

Luckily, Dittmer was big and strong. He took Maria in his arms and carried her out the back door of the depot. There, a car was waiting and the driver helped Dittmer lay her in the back seat.

"Thank you," the driver said and they shook hands. "God will bless you for your help, my son."

He hugged Dittmer friendly and handed him a wad of bills.

"This is from parishioners of my Cathedral," he explained.

Twenty minutes later Maria woke up, feeling someone slightly patting her cheek. She opened her eyes and was overwhelmed by a bright blue light. The man who was looking down at her was dressed in a black cassock. His hair was graying (Maria guessed he was about sixty) and his face shone with kindness and compassion.

"Are you a priest?" she managed to say. "What is all this blue? Am I already in heaven?"

"You seem to still have your sense of humor, my daughter," the priest laughed. "That's a good sign. I am Father Jorgen Launer and you are in St. Peter's Cathedral. You are safe here, but don't wander outside without me.

"The West Berlin, where we are now, is free. But it's the only a half of the city of Berlin. We're still in the middle of the Communist East Germany. So their Communist Secret Police agents – Stasi – whom, I'm sure, you know quite well, sneaking even into our part of the city, looking for refugees. Stasi have their special undercover tunnels under Berlin Wall and walking through them, here and back, very easily, like they are at home. They're absolutely impertinent, feeling free to search even the West Berlin. They could point the newcomers from East, like you, in a moment; then grab you and return home. They, possibly, are already having your picture.

"You'd better wait here, inside the church about a month, until your papers for immigration to the U.S. are ready."

"Yes, Father. Whatever you say," Maria looked at him thankfully.

She wasn't a religious person. She'd grown up in an atheistic family and educated in a Communist regime which didn't recognize, and even prohibited, any kind of religious expression. However now, seeing this caring man and hearing the tender concern in his voice, Maria experienced some sort of holy feelings. Who was she to him? Just another human being; just a *daughter*. Her gratitude and respect toward him was evident for his sincere assistance.

"How can I locate my husband?" Maria wanted to know. "He's supposed to come today on a delta plane. Another group is helping him: Otto and Franz. Do you know them?"

Father Jorgen smiled and nodded. "We have a meeting point where your husband will land. Don't worry, my dear. He'll be here tonight."

"Can I go with you to meet him?" Maria asked hopefully.

"Better not, my dear. You take a shower, eat something, then relax and sleep. Let's go now. I'll show you your room in the basement where you can take care of yourself. Last night you went through a lot and deserve a rest. But I'll be going myself and will drive your husband back here. I know what to do. Believe me; I've been doing this for many years."

Maria dutifully went down the stairs to her room. She knew she could trust this priest.

After her shower and a quick bite to eat, she laid down. Her mind was tense with anticipation and, at the moment, there was nothing harder to bear than that. She closed her weary lids and saw her husband in her mind's eye.

I love you, Peter. Please, arrive safely, she silently pleaded with him. Please, I'm waiting for you…

Maria turned to Nick once more and pointed out another picture, "Here is the image about my husband - the cherry one."

Nick swiveled his head and looked at the painting on the wall behind him. It combined lines and points and lightening that twisted and dissolved in tones of cherry, soft pink and fuchsia. It portrayed one more miracle in Maria's life.

"I'm not sure if I can really talk about him," she commented wistfully. "I'll try, but if I can't, please, don't feel offended. The subject is sacred and very private for me. Actually, I have to admit, I don't know why I'm sharing all this with you at all."

Maria knew, however, why she was doing it. It was for Alana's sake, to keep Nick here longer; to entertain him until her daughter came home at last. Being ready to sacrifice herself for Alana's possible happiness, she was convinced that, if Nick had come here, he must want to see her daughter about something important.

Maria glanced at the clock once more. It was already about nine. She took a deep breath and returned to her narrative.

"Do you know why this cherry color is here? I always considered Peter as a cherry. He was my sweet cherry. I don't know why, but I just felt it."

... Maria had been waiting for hours. It made her tired. In the small room there was nothing to do but lay down, eyes closed, and recall her life with her husband.

She had met Peter Miller during her first year at Humboldt University where both of them were studying journalism. In a year they were married. They had now been together twenty years, but their love was as fresh as their first encounter.

For East Germans, they both were blessed with amazing careers. Peter was the political columnist of the leading newspaper *Neues Deutschland*, while Maria was a news correspondent at the same paper. They both circulated among the cream of society, and had a variety of prestigious and fascinating friends and interesting and well-paid work.

Everything was picture-perfect in their lives, except for one thing – their phones were always bugged. They were under the Stasi's constant surveillance, but it was normal for East Germany and seldom bothered them.

In their years of marriage, Maria and Peter had had no children, and gave little thought to why. Anyway, their lives were too full and busy for children; they lived in a whirlwind of meeting foreign delegations, international conferences, business travel, the Olympics, and opening nights at the theater. This vortex of activity excited them and drew on their creativity and intelligence. They were the best of friends, co-workers and lovers. They happily and confidently moved along this trajectory until one fateful day, when this world suddenly collapsed.

They must leave. They should run away; escape. Everything was over here, anyway. There was nothing to lose anymore. Danger surrounded them and they must take a chance to save their lives. The night of Maria's departure was their last night together, their last kisses and lovemaking.

She was crying in Peter's arms, caressing his neck and molding her trembling body to his.

"I love you, Peter. I love you madly. I love you forever," she whispered through her choking tears. "I couldn't live without you, darling."

He was stronger than she was. He held himself in check and studiously suppressed his own fears.

"Don't say such things, sweetie," he admonished her. "What are you talking about, anyway? Why should you have to live without me? Don't worry. We are only going to be apart for some hours, less than a day, really. We'll be together tomorrow night, for sure."

Maria sensed that it was all a front. The cells of his body communicated his real uncertainty and fear of the unknown that lay ahead of them. They had a fifty-fifty chance of both making it across the border to safety. A moment of life and death stood before them. It would all be decided by fate.

"You've never loved me as totally as you did today," Peter softly kissed her shoulders and tender breasts. "And I've never been so much in love with you as now." He lovingly sucked her full pink nipples and laughed. "Our baby is supposed to do that, not me. It's probably the only think in our live that I regret. We should have had a baby. We should live someone in the world after us. What we wrote for the newspaper won't last. Those articles are like dust in the wind and will mean nothing."

"Don't say that," Maria objected. "What would we do now, if we had a child? How could we take him with us? It would be impossible!"

"Maybe if we had a child, out whole life would be different, and this wouldn't be happening."

"No," Maria protested. "No, no, my love. Everything happened because of Albert. You know that. A child couldn't possibly have been a part of it. And don't regret anything. I was happy before…and I'm happy with you now. And we'll be happy together in the future, too, no matter where or how we live. I just need to know that we'll always be together. That's all."

At three o'clock in the morning Maria had left with Klaus. On the first train at five-thirty she rode into West Berlin, cramped inside the black box under the carriage.

"Why did you travel separately?" Nick wanted to know.

"Well, Peter was big and tall, and too heavy to hang under the carriage. He couldn't fit in a box. They found another way for him, something new then, called a delta plane. The smugglers were always looking for new ways to get people over, under or through the Wall. These delta planes were not perfected or a hundred percent.

"They located a tall building near the Wall and they were able to bribe the guars there. Helpers got the folded plane up to the roof, somehow. There they opened it out and attached Peter to it. He was supposed to run and jump and sort of glide about a quarter of a mile and land in the park on the West Berlin side of the Wall. I guess there was some miss-timing of the border patrol. Or perhaps the patrol was at random. I don't know exactly, but Peter was quickly spotted and soldiers shot him in flight. His plane landed with his limp body. Father Jorgen brought it back to the Cathedral so I saw him one more time."

Maria's voice broke. "Sorry I can't talk any more about it," she spoke in husky tones. "This painting tried to capture that chapter."

She pointed at the canvas, stood up and then retreated to her bed-room, leaving Nick alone.

After ten minutes Maria reappeared. She had washed her face with cold water and changed into black pants and blouse, and now had black slippers on her feet.

Nick had remained seated on the couch. He was attempting to soak up the atmosphere of the paintings and match them to the story he had been privileged to hear.

It was already ten-thirty. The night was darkening outside into a deep blue and filling the living room with mystery.

"Sorry," Maria said. "It's getting dark. Shall I turn on more lights?"

"No, it's not necessary," Nick answered, shaking his head. "I like it this way. Diffused light from the street is better and offers a better set-ting for your pictures. I encountered them once before this way, and the sensation has stayed with me."

"You've seen them before? Sorry, I don't really understand..." Maria knitted her brows, puzzled.

"Oh, nothing," Nick laughed it off. Obviously, she didn't know a thing about the night he spent here with Alana a week ago. It was impor-tant to him that she not knew about it.

"Alana is still out, I'm afraid," Maria noted. "I honestly didn't expect this. She has been home every evening this week. But sometimes she needs to go out and relax with her friends. You should understand that. She's young and she works hard."

"It's okay," Nick wanted to reassure her. "I can come another time."

"I'm so sorry you had to waste a whole evening here. Alana tells me you're very busy these days."

"Sometimes."

"Your time is money," Maria continued, with a hint of sarcasm.

"Are you trying to get rid of me?" Nick laughed. "Sorry, I know, I tore you away from your painting."

"It's okay. My time is not money. I can do it later."

"Thank you for teasing," Nick smirked, bitterly. "Anyway, I won't leave until I know all about your paintings. There are still unanswered questions, black holes so to speak. And, who knows, maybe Alana will finally come."

"I hope so," Maria answered softly. "Do you want to know what happened with us? The happy journalists from Berlin? This painting is about that. It's about my brother."

...Albert and Maria were born to parents in the Communist leadership. European history and politics were mixed with their blood. Their fates – the ups and downs – were predestined by their births.

Their father, Richard Franzke, took part in the first German Communist uprising in 1918. After it failed, the organization was forced underground and Richard spent much time in hiding. His life was filled with risks and dangerous adventures; a man living on a knife-edge.

Some years later he married a party comrade, Sofia, who had actively fought the German government. They continued their political struggles together and, in 1930, Albert was born.

No one imaged that things could get much worse, yet just three years later Adolph Hitler, the world beast, came to power. Most of the German Communists were rounded up and many were murdered. It looked like a dead-end for the Franzke family.

However, someone was watching out for Richard and Sofia and they were miraculously able to flee over the Alps to neutral Switzerland. The trip was intensely arduous; the three of them, guided by a local, passed over rough and dangerous mountain trails. In his backpack, Richard carried the precious cargo of little Albert, while in her backpack Sofia carried their communist activity documents.

As refugee, the Franzke family led a simple, modest life in Bern and carried on their political activism. Maria joined their family in 1940.

In this period, Richard maintained his close ties with the Russian Communist Party and the Comintern. By the end of the bloody Second World War, Russian troops occupied the Eastern half of Germany. As soon as this news reached them, the Franzkes, under the thunder of the final high-explosive shells, quickly returned to Berlin. The Russians didn't hesitate to appoint Richard to one of the highest positions in the newly-formed East German government.

Albert was fifteen and Maria just five, when the family was catapulted to the elite spheres of political life. They were surrounded by well-connected, wealthy families that formed the new high society. From then on, they were comfortable and happy and the way forward looked just as smooth and straight as one could ever ask for. With Soviet backing, their father's and family's position was secure.

Maria and Albert didn't play together much in childhood because of the age gap, but they still loved one another fiercely and devotedly. Albert thought of Maria as a cute little doll; she saw him as a hero and mimicked his every move.

Maria ran after Albert, always trying to keep up with her big brother. She often fell and scratched or bruised herself and sometimes cried, but it didn't matter. She worshipped him and strove to be with and like him.

Both of them were smart and talented kids. They easily grasped their school lessons and learned the ropes of life, as well. Maria has reached just the age of ten, when Albert was already a Humboldt University student who took journalism. He was good at writing and prepared to become a loyal communist journalist, being convinced that his political regime was the best in the world. No wonder, it really was for him.

Only one phone call from his father to the Minister of the Education was enough for Albert to be enrolled into university courses. It was a huge privilege at the Communist countries. The education there was free, but the young people had to compete with each other for placement – the exams were extremely difficult and failure to get in could result in living in a lower class society. At the time when about 20-30 people applied for one place at university Albert got it effortlessly, without any competition.

So, another phone call was made, and Albert was appointed the Chief of the Economics Department at the newspaper *Neues Deutschland* following graduation at twenty-four. It was a position that many experienced newsman could only dream of after twenty or twenty-five years of professional experience. However, Albert walked right to the post and hung up his hat.

In spite of his easy access, Albert applied himself to both his education and doing a good job. He ruled his department well with organizational skills, attention to detail and even - handedness. In fact, everyone liked Albert and was happy to work with him.

Maria determined to follow in her brother's footsteps. When their father died, Albert took his sister under his wing. She and her husband, Peter Miller, also graduated in journalism, so now Albert made a couple of phone calls and found easily two positions for them at *Neues Deutschland*.

For fifteen years they continued working together and had a best life imaginable for a Communist country. However, it was all to come crashing down after Albert joined a delegation to the Soviet Union for a regular plenary session of the Communist Party in Moscow.

It was both an honor and a privilege to travel to the Kremlin, because it was the true center of power for all Eastern Europe. Of course, Albert was fluent in Russian and had visited Russia before. This trip he spent a week and it was to change his life forever.

He flew back to Berlin, arriving late at night. Maria and Peter had already turned in for the night when Albert called them from the airport and said that he needed to talk to them immediately, would take a taxi and come to their suite in a half-an-hour. Peter heard the obvious worry in Albert's voice and understood the seriousness of the occasion.

They dressed right away; then Maria brewed some strong coffee and set the table. Albert came in nervous and ashen. In the entrance he requested that Maria unplug their telephones. Peter and Maria grasped in a wink that he would speak about politics.

"You know, my dear friends," Albert began hesitantly, "I have an announcement to make: We live here in a rotten, stinking swamp and have no idea what is going on in the world. In the Soviet Union a new underground opposition has emerged."

"That's impossible," Peter responded, wrinkling his forehead in disbelief. "It couldn't happen."

"It's true, Peter. I accidentally ran into them. They were trying to reach some foreign journalists to get their message out. I talked to them a lot. They took me to meet a pretty famous academician in radiation physics who's leading their group. He's a Nobel prizewinner, you know, so I'm sure you've heard of him. He's really an amazing man, a short, weak and frail, but his spirit is so strong! He reminded me of someone like Jesus Christ: intelligent, soulful and compassionate. I have to admit that he completely turned my mind upside down and inside out. He managed to open my eyes about politics, economics and corruption.

"He passed me his book manuscript and asked me to help him get it to the West for publication. Before I do, I want very much for you to read it. Intellectuals should understand how blind we've all been, living like newborn kittens."

Maria and Peter were overwhelmed by the sudden shakeup of their thinking.

"Albert, are you sure the KGB didn't follow you?" Maria asked. "Don't you think that everyone in the opposition would be under close surveillance?"

"I'm sure they are. The KGB might already have transferred my file to the Stasi. That's why I want you to hide the manuscript for awhile. They very likely will search me and my place."

"Do you really understand the danger you're courting?" Peter wanted to know. "You don't realize…"

"Oh, I do. But it doesn't matter now. I can't live anymore like I used to. Really, everything that I did before was totally pointless, false and destructive. We've been burying our heads in the sand like a bunch of ostriches, pretending not to know, or see the plain truth. We preferred not to face the fact that the Communist system is bankrupt and degenerate, because we had certain privileges. We kept our mouths shut and continued filling our newspaper with lies because we were well-paid. I can see now that I was merely prostituting myself by writing propaganda.

"Well, it's over for me. I'm making break with it. I've already gone over to the opposition and I'll be with them till the day I die."

Pained by these revelations, Maria protested, "You'll be sent to prison. Oh, Albert, I don't want that!"

"Don't worry. I'll escape to the West. I already have contacts with smugglers here, in Berlin, who was helping people get out. Maybe you could say I got this opposition streak from our dad, to fight the state on principle and be ready for political exile.

"All that I'm asking of you is to read the book, hide it, and return it to me when I leave. And be ready to change your lives."

When Albert had gone home, Maria and Peter poured over the manuscript all night long. They found it disturbing and full of explosive charges, like a minefield. By the time they came to the end of it, they understood Albert better. Around 5 A.M. they carefully wrapped it in plastic and slipped it between the walls of their wardrobe. It was only a matter of time before their own secure existence would crumble, and fear and tension would replace the certainty they had long enjoyed. They, like Albert, had a lot to lose, but, then again, they had a new reality to gain.

The Stasi were no slackers and worked surprisingly fast. The next morning Albert was fired from his job. Within a week he retrieved the book and was smuggled into West Berlin through a sewer tunnel, aided by Klaus and Father Jorgen. Maria saw him off and got contacts with Klaus just in case she would need to leave quickly herself.

For the time being, nobody touched Peter and Maria; they continued their life and work as usual. The only thing that happened was they got an invitation to visit Stasi Headquarters.

The building itself was dark gray, huge and gloomy. As she entered, Maria felt feverish, not to mention, scared. She couldn't be sure they'd ever be allowed to leave so she nervously clasped Peter's strong hand. His fingers answered hers and gave her strength to fight her fears.

They were ushered into a big office and found themselves surrounded by cold walls adorned with portraits of Communist bosses – both German and Russian. Maria noticed that her father's picture had been removed.

From the double doors, a long narrow red-striped carpet led to a heavy oak table at the far end. There sat one official with military bearing and a bleak face with no personality, who stared at them with his water-colored empty eyes.

"Frau Miller! Tell me why was your brother betrayed his Motherland?" he began brusquely, without any greetings or prelude.

Maria stood silently, pressing her lips. She knew very well there was no reason to replay; anyway he wouldn't be listening to her answer. Motionless, she continued looking unconsciously at the man's face, waiting dutifully until he'd completed his lecture.

My God, she thought, why should Peter have to suffer with me?

The man reprimanded them both sternly, as if they were guilty schoolchildren. He reminded Maria about her once-respected family, her university, her social position, her work, and even reminded her that she had failed to produce any children. Everything was made to appear soiled and besmirched, especially her close relationship with Albert. Maria might as well have been put on a torture rack. They had no choice but to endure this lengthy humiliation and accusation and register none of the outrage welling up inside them. After 'obediently' listening for forty-five minutes, they were directly instructed to forget Albert ever lived. They must cut off all relations with him.

Peter was especially advised that if Maria made even one mistake in this regard, he should divorce her right away in order to keep his position at the newspaper.

Chastened and stunned, they stumbled from the headquarters and sat for awhile in their parked car. Peter was unable to drive because his hands were shaking and Maria sobbed hysterically, hanging on his neck. He was surprised by her outburst – this was a side of her he had never seen in twenty years. From now on it wouldn't be her last fit of hysteria.

After three month Albert phoned Maria from West Berlin, to again say goodbye. His immigration papers to the U.S. were ready. He wanted to hear her voice one last time. Both of them shed tears at the final separation.

The next morning, Maria was fired from *Neues Deutschland*. A week later, Peter's turn came to get the sack. Then the Stasi evicted them from their deluxe suite.

From one of their friends they soon found a small room to rent, but the Stasi continued to follow them. The people who were helping Maria and Peter began having difficulties and, before long, refused any further contact with them. They were becoming 'persona non grate' and found themselves out on the street.

The last card they had to play was to appeal to Maria's mother, Frau Sofia Franzke. Maria had hesitated to take this step until the very last, since her mother, now eighty, was still very bossy and sharp. The widowed Sofia continued to live in the big beautiful family apartment in a government building. In spite of her advanced age, she led an active social life and was at the forefront of her circle of friends – all of them retired Communist officials.

Sofia was not close to her children. Motherhood came late in her life and she was already a public figure more used to political activity than childcare and housework.

When they returned from Switzerland to Germany and got high position at the society, she always had maids and nannies for Maria. Naturally, she was proud of her children's achievements, but usually saw them no more than a couple of times a year.

Sofia's apartment was bugged like everyone else's, but that wasn't the main reason Maria didn't want to report to her about the results of Albert's defection. She was fairly sure her mother would find it all scandalous and perhaps damn her own son and daughter for any connection to dissidents.

However, now Maria really had no choice. She needed to make everything perfectly clear to her mother, but she looked forward to it like a condemned person does the executioner's block.

As Maria entered the familiar family suite, she saw her bent mother hobble toward her, propped up by a cane. Her arthritis was probably getting worse today.

"I know everything, girl," Sofia spoke abruptly before Maria could even open her mouth. "They were here a couple of hours ago. They're all dogs! They tried to scare me! Pieces of shit! I told them to piss off!" She made a hideous face, depicting the Stasi. "'How come, Frau Franzke, your son betrayed his Motherland? Is that how you raised him?' Do you know what I told them, girl?" Sofia cackled with disdain, "I said, 'When my husband was alive, you bastards followed him, kissed his footprints and wanted to kiss his ass, dreaming to gain by it. And now you're trying to say my son is not good. No way!' I threw my cane at them as hard as I could and ordered them to get out! Can you imagine that, girl? I hit them and they ran away."

Laughing victoriously, Sofia threw her arms around her startled daughter. In so doing, she nudged her back toward the front door.

"But, girl, there's no way for you to stay in my suite. You should go, just go, just go!"

Maria sensed that her mother had thrust something into her coat pocket and squeezed her hands.

"Thank you, Mom," she whispered, kissed Sofia's flabby cheek and left.

Only out on the street did she dare investigate to see what had been placed in her pocket. It was just a little piece of paper which read, "Here is address of Gertrude, my cleaning lady. She lives on a farm and will hide you."

Thus, Sofia presented them with a few months of shelter and existence below the Stasi's radar. It was the only thing she could really do for her younger child and, at the same time, protect herself. Even this small thing was priceless for them, but it couldn't last long. It was simply too dangerous to remain in East Germany.

Maria and Peter were now on a list of enemies of the state and 'accidents' easily happened to such people. One day they just disappeared and were effortlessly killed or thrown in a prison or a mental institution. Things could only get worse. It was clearly time to run. All their sources of survival were drying up and they were being hunted high and low by the police as dangerous criminals. Their time was up...

"This painting is about our life in hiding," Maria redirected Nick's attention. "Can you understand the feelings?"

Wordlessly, he nodded to her.

"I did hear something about that," he murmured, "but I didn't pay much attention when Alana told me. I didn't understand what she was talking about."

When he was in the hospital Alana had poured out her parents' story, but, wrapped in his own pain, he failed to really listen. Now, he was dumbfounded. From the painting he got the horrible sense of constantly being watched, chased, threatened and hunted down.

Nick really couldn't imagine a life without freedom, with bugged phones, with spies always ready to tail you. He couldn't even picture himself – or his father – sneaking through a sewer tunnel, hiding in a box under a train carriage, or jumping from a building strapped to a delta plane. That certainly took desperation – and courage. Although some things that were dangerous appeared on the TV show *Fear Factor*, that was all staged and used safety nets. What happened to Peter and Maria was true danger and had resulted in a real death.

While Nick had been caught up in Maria's compelling story, he felt uncomfortable and a little ashamed. Here were people who had to risk everything, though they were innocent, just to survive! Compare that with his indulgent, pampered world here in Minneapolis, he could now see why Alana argued he had no right to give up on life. Nick was so worked up that he had to fight the desire to kneel at Maria's feet and kiss her hands like a Madonna. Instead, he silently concentrated on her artwork.

"I haven't told you about this last painting yet," Maria continued. "These are the mosaic windows of St. Peter's Cathedral in West Berlin. In the mornings, the sun flooded in through the newly build blue glass wall and bathed the entire chapel in the most beautiful blue color. In the afternoons the sun had shifted, and from other side, through the original antique mosaic windows, turned the white marble floor multicolored. Peter is buried there…"

Maria lived in the cathedral basement for two months awaiting her papers. After receiving Peter's corpse she was unable to cry and existed in a zombie state without feeling or reactions. She spent days on end sitting or lying without engaging with the life around her. She barely ate, though Father Jorgen and his sister, Anna, spent a lot of time with her and tried to care for her. They found it impossible to alleviate her grief and isolation. They would often find her wandering around the cathedral for hours, absorbed in the blue and colored light of the sanctuary.

Every day, the priest and Anna walked Maria to a nearby park and taught her to pick wild cranberries and cook the juice. It was the only nourishment she didn't refuse. She drank a lot of cranberry juice and it sustained her. She liked it because it sobered her and gradually brought her back to the real world.

On Maria's fortieth birthday, her immigration papers were ready. Both these events were cause for celebration and Father Jorgen announced them at service. The parishioners brought a lot of gifts for Maria, hoping that they would make her a bit happier.

Soon it was time to go. All Maria's presents were packed in a bag along with some of her new clothes Anna bought for her. Father Jorgen handed Maria $500 cash and drove her to the airport. She was handed over to the flight attendant there for special care on her flight.

"God bless you, my dear child," he said as he gave her a farewell hug. "You will start your new life from ground zero, but I hope it will be better and happier life than you had here. Keep in touch, please, if you can."

During the eleven-hour flight, Maria felt nauseous most of the time. After landing in New York, she went straight to the restroom where she vomited for the next ten minutes. Then she washed her face and examined herself in the mirror. She really looked terrible. She had lost lots of weight, her face was drained of color and she had huge black circles under her eyes.

It suddenly came to Maria that she hadn't had a period for two months, so she might be pregnant. Here she was: widowed, alone in an unknown country at age forty with little money, no home, no friends, no job, and no knowledge of English at all. And now she was probably carrying her first child!

Through U.S. customs she carried two other things besides the tiny embryo in her womb: Albert's phone number – her lifeline to the future, and Peter's photo – her connection to the past...

"It's already completely dark and you can't see anything," Maria said to Nick as she switched on the table lamp. "There is a couple more images left of my early life in America. They were equally hard to paint, but we don't have time for them now. Please, don't say or think I'm trying to get rid of you, but it's almost midnight. Alana will probably come home very late. She sometimes goes to a club until closing time.

"I'm tired now and need to get some sleep. Sorry about that. I've been working very hard and don't have any helpers these days. Albert, as you know, is dying and my other helper, my 'adopted son', is currently serving in Afghanistan. So, I really need my rest."

"You don't have to apologize," Nick stood, stretched and slowly made his way to the door. "I should be the one to say sorry because I took so much of your time this evening. And I can see that sharing all those things hasn't been easy for you. So, I'm really sorry. Please forgive me. I just needed interpretation to understand and feel your special art. In fact, this evening has been the most wonderful I've ever had. And don't worry about helpers. I'll come by and help you."

"Thank you," Maria graciously shook his hand and he left.

She couldn't count on a man like that, but was happy about one thing: it looked like Nick was serious about her Alana.

Hadn't he spent the whole evening hearing about her family and waiting for her? Maria thought. Hopefully, these hours will prove profitable in some way. It's good for him to have a taste of Alana's background, even though I paid the price to relieve all those memories! I feel tired and almost sick now. However, Alana was right saying that he is an unusual and very handsome man. He seems to be both spiritual and talented.

Alana appeared half-an-hour later, smiling, and smelled of beer and cigarette smock. Maria was very sleepy but went into the kitchen to talk to her.

"Where were you for so long?" she asked impatiently.

"What's the problem, Mom? Jessica and Samantha came by St. Boniface's to meet me after work. We had dinner then went to the club. Do you remember Bob, one of Tom's friends? Well, he's back from Kabul because he was wounded. He brought me a letter from Tom. Do you want to read it? Tom asked me to kiss you for him."

Alana kissed Maria's cheek and bubbled with laughter.

"I'm glad you're in such a good mood. But the problem is that..." Maria paused to convey the seriousness of her announcement, "...your Nick was here this evening waiting for you. He came at seven and I tried to keep him here for you for some time. He wanted to talk to you, probably something important, but you didn't come or call. Finally, he left, but he promised to come again."

"That's really strange," Alana said. "Why didn't he call first?"

"It seemed strange to me, too," Maria agreed. "But what should I have done? I showed him my paintings – I was working on one when he came – and I told him some stories, as well. Please, Alana you need to be home more often."

"No, Mom," Alana objected, lifting up her head proudly. "Ab-so-lute-ly not! I talked to my girlfriends tonight and told them about Nick. They gave me lots of good advice. I was making many mistakes with Nick, trying to run after him and always pushing myself in his face. Jessica explained that handsome men who know their own value just run away from that type of girl. So, from now on, you won't find me waiting at home for him to phone. Instead, I'll let him suffer and chase after me. It's more fun that way, anyway. You'll see. It'll work."

Chapter 7

THE NEXT MORNING, AFTER ALANA left for work, Maria began her chores around the building.

She changed the tapes in both security camera systems, indoors and out, took a reading from the gauges in the mechanical room and checked the machines for leaks. Then she went out into the morning air and watered the petunias in the garden and picked up the litter on the lawn.

Next Maria walked over to the parking garage to check if most of the occupants had already gone for the day, so she could began cleaning there. She exchanged the full trash bags for clean ones in the cans on each floor by the stairs and prepared a pail of hot water to mop the lobby and back hallways.

When she came to the entrance lobby, mop in hand, she suddenly saw Nick standing in the foyer between the main doors. She stood her mop and pail in the corner and went to open the door for him.

Oh, gosh. He missed Alana again, she thought. What a shame!

Nick was dressed more casually today, wearing blue jeans and a simple gray T-shirt. He stood with his hands in his pockets, looking at her.

"Good morning, Maria," he greeted her when she opened the door and flashed at her a smile. He seemed more carefree and confident than the previous evening.

"Good morning, Nick," she answered, but without stepping aside for him to pass. "Alana left for work about an hour ago. I'm sorry, but you missed her for a second time."

"Really?" he laughed. "It must be fate. So, what is left for me? Well, since I'm here, could I run my eyes over your paintings again? They must look different in daylight."

"Hmmm. Actually, I need to get to work this morning," Maria was confused. "It's going to be a busy day. I'm sorry I can't show them to you right now."

"Oh-oh…I did promise to help you," he said. "Well, I'm ready and at your service. Just tell me what to do."

"Are you joking? You don't want to help in truth, do you? Do you have any idea what a resident manager does?"

"Not really," Nick admitted and laughed. "Cleaning? Organizing things? You can train me…"

"Well, Mr. Nick. You absolutely don't need to know," Maria protested, shaking her head. "This kind of work is beneath you."

"Nothing is beneath me. This job is part of life, so I want to know everything."

Maria shook her head again in disbelieve.

"Okay," she agreed merrily to test him. "The man's duties for this job are to change the light bulbs if they are very high and I can't reach them, to mow the lawn, to shovel show around the building and wash the underground garage in winter."

"Okay. Let's go change light bulbs, then," Nick suggested, ready for action.

"There aren't any burnt out ones right now," Maria objected, amused. He was really like a boy, after all: kind of enthusiastic and charming.

"Okay, how about mowing the lawn? I used to do it when I was a teenager. I know how."

"I'm afraid it was done just a couple of days ago. Thanks, Nick, but there is nothing for you to do today."

"Oh, poor me," he said, playfully exaggerating his miserable state. "You're really trying to get rid of me, aren't you? Well, then…I want my cranberry juice, first. You did promise I can have some every day."

"I did not," Maria teased back gently. "You were the one who said you wanted it. I made no promises."

"Well, then let me keep my promise to have some everyday."

"Okay. You win," Maria yielded, tickled by his persistence. "Come in and I'll give you your juice."

She allowed him to step into the lobby and follow her to her suite.

This time when she poured him the cranberry juice, she left it on the table, rather than hand it to him. She quickly withdrew her hand when Nick took the glass.

Smiling, he looked straight into her eyes and asked, "Did I scare you yesterday with the glass? I'm sorry. It was just my little joke."

Slowly, he swallowed the crimson juice, stretching out each sip with the glass against his lower lip.

"It's amazing," he told her, as he returned the empty glass. "Can you please give me your recipe? Or better yet, teach me how to make it?"

"I have no time," Maria objected.

"That's okay. I can remind you later. Just promise me you will."

86

Maria laughed. He seemed really intent on pursuing it and she found his interest flattering.

"Yes," she said. "My recipes aren't state secrets or anything. I can share it with you some other time. But now…I'm really sorry; I can't stand around and talk. I must get back to work. I need to finish here so I can visit my brother and talk to his doctor about the surgery. So, you see, I'll be tied up the whole day."

"Is the hospital far?"

She nodded.

"I can drive you there. Actually, I'd find it very interesting to meet your brother. From what you told me about him yesterday, I'd say he's a pretty remarkable guy. This may be my only chance to meet him. Pleeese?"

"I'll go to the hospital right after lunch," Maria raised another objection. "But now I must get to work."

"I already heard that," Nick laughed. "Well, if there's no work for me then maybe I can just stay here and look at your paintings while I wait a few hours for you. You don't have to worry. I'm not a burglar."

"There is nothing to steel here, anyway," Maria said, confused. "But I don't understand. You probably need to get to work. You must have something you need to do today."

"My business just takes care of itself. Or rather, I'm on vacation."

"Well it's already ten o'clock. I should get back to work. I'll return about noon. Oh, and don't answer the phone. People are supposed to leave messages. Okay, then. Relax and enjoy the paintings. There's more cranberry juice in the fridge. See you later."

Maria went out and left Nick behind alone in her suite.

He is certainly a very strange man, she thought, but genuine. Maybe he is seriously in love with Alana. It's moving that he wants to know more about the family and even meet Albert. Not every potential son-in-law would be ready to drive me to the hospital. I appreciated his offer of help. Actually, Tom wasn't so bad in this department, but he worked a lot and was usually too busy.

Today some owners were renovating their condos and that always created a huge mess in the building. Workers pulled rolls of old carpets from the elevators and dragged them through the back hallways to the loading dock door. As a result the elevators and hall floors were messed with chalk, paint and bits, and pieces of carpeting and underlay foam. The glass doors were all smeared with grease, creating extra work for Maria.

She got back to her apartment about one o'clock, tired, dusty and sweaty.

Maria didn't want to show Nick her exhaustion, so she quietly slipped down the corridor to the bathroom. There, she showered, dressed, and put on a little make-up. After a minute she decided to use the last drops in her *Lily of the Valley* perfume bottle. It was by Dior and her favorite. Maria bought it some years ago for herself after saving money for several months. It was quite expensive and now it would be impossible to afford a replacement. She had taken all of her savings to help Albert with his cancer treatment.

She was dressed in a long black skirt with big brown flowers, black top and black slip-ons on her feet.

Why am I dressing up like this? Maria asked herself as she looked in the mirror. He didn't come to see me. Well, it's still better not to be ugly and sloppy. That could push him away from Alana. I know that men usually try to check out their girl's mother so they can see what their wife will look like further down the road.

Now, what can I prepare for lunch? I don't have much on hand. Maybe there are a couple of hotdogs left in the freezer...

She went to the kitchen and hesitated at the entrance, startled by what she found.

There, the humble kitchen table was decked out in a white silk tablecloth and set with silver. A large white rose in a vase graced the center, surrounded by three small candles in silver holders. On the kitchen counter stood a big, lidded silver serving bowl - Maria could smell something delicious inside. Nick stood beside the table, organizing the linen napkins and fine china plates, trying to fit everything on the small table. He turned to greet Maria.

"Sorry, I made myself at home," he said a little embarrassed. "I got hungry and I knew you were working so hard you probably wouldn't want to cook. I'm not a big cook, either. So, I took the liberty of ordering lunch from *Astoria*. I kept menu simple, like mushroom soup and some sandwiches. They delivered it half an hour ago so it's still hot. Sit down, please, won't you?"

Nick gallantly pulled out the chair for her and stood behind it. Maria, too, was embarrassed by all the fuss.

"My gosh!" she exclaimed, covering her eyes with her hand. "How can I ever return the favor?"

"You don't have to. I'm trying to pay you back for everything you gave me last night: your paintings, your stories, your talent, your soul... even your cranberry juice. I could never fully repay you for all that. You opened up to me so much..." he sincerely told her, then lightened up. "Well, that's enough of that. I'm hungry. Let's eat!"

"Thank you," Maria responded and chuckled, "You can probably tell that I'm as hungry as a wolf."

During their lunch, Maria finished relating her life story to Nick. They were the details about her happy reunion with her brother Albert and his new bride, Luisa. They had met at the German Community Center in Minneapolis soon after he had arrived the year before. Luisa owned the German grocery and deli *Berlin* on the north side of the city. Albert started to work in her store, mainly because it was the only job he could get at age fifty with no English skills. Luisa was already sick with multiple sclerosis at the time and would later need a wheelchair for mobility. In spite of her disability, she and Albert helped Maria a lot, especially in bringing up Alana.

Maria almost had no time at all for her only child. She held two jobs and was always running between them, putting in 12-13 hours a day to make ends meet.

"I did work at a German restaurant bussing tables and washing dishes," she said. "I also worked as a housekeeper in different hotels. I even – you will laugh – worked at the *Astoria* for two years. That was about fifteen years ago.

"At Christmas parties there, I would see your father. He usually came to the employee party and greeted us all. One of his nephews was with him once, but it wasn't you. I would remember if you had been there."

"Why do you say that?" asked Nick. "Am I so remarkable?"

"I think so," Maria admitted softly. "It sure is interesting how small the world is."

"I definitely wasn't there," Nick confirmed. "That's when I was at Harvard. Of course, Gary and I came home for the holidays some years, but usually on Christmas Eve."

"I also saw your father last year, when he bought *West-Build Management*. He came here with a group of three or four engineers and property managers to tour the building and to do a maintenance check. This building belongs to *West-Build Management*. Did you know that?"

Nick shook his head as he finished his soup and ham sandwich, "But I realize it now." He gave her a big, wide grin.

"So I saw your father, but, of course, he didn't really notice me. I'm not offended by it. It's perfectly understandable. Again, you weren't with him."

"I think that happened when I was deliriously happy that I had finished my book and was pretty far from the business end of things."

"I'm just noting that for many years our paths almost crossed, since we were connected in some way," Maria continued, "but we never met until... until *that* happened to you. Then you met Alana at the hospital in such a miserable state..."

"And then I met you," Nick added slowly, looking straight into her eyes.

"That's not so important," she protested.

"It is for me."

"Well..." Maria stood up. "Thank you for an amazing lunch, Nick. It was a pleasant surprise. I never expected it. But now, we must go to the hospital to see Albert. What are we going to do with all these nice things?"

"You can keep them all. They're already paid for," Nick explained.

"But that's not necessary. We have our own dishes and all," Maria politely objected. "Can't we just return them to the restaurant?"

"No way," Nick laughed. "I want you to always serve me lunches on silk with silver. They're my favorite."

"Hmmm... well..." she replied warily.

For two days following his surgery, Albert had been in the intensive care ward. Now, though, he had been transferred back to a regular ward where he could receive visitors. He was still on oxygen and IV, but he was smiling when they arrived and could talk a little.

"Hi, big brother. How are you?" Maria said as she kissed both his cheeks and hands in greeting.

"Hi, little dolly," Albert voiced his words huskily. He looked up at Nick with a question mark on his face.

"Oh, Albert, sorry. This is Nick. He's Alana's...Alana's friend."

"Nice to meet you," Albert managed a polite acknowledgement. "I saw Alana before my surgery. She came by for a visit. I have to tell you she is my sweetheart." His voice broke and he asked for a drink of water before continuing. "She promised to name her first son 'Albert' after me. Is that all right with you, Nick?"

"It's too soon to talk about that," Nick answered, feeling he'd been put on the spot. "For now, I just wanted to meet you, Albert. I've heard a lot about you from Maria. You are truly living history. Actually, I'm not too bad in history, but I don't know so much about Germany and the Berlin Wall. Maria was telling me some things yesterday. And I'd be happy to talk with you more when you're feeling better."

"Oh, if you're interested in politics, young man, I could tell you a lot," Albert perked up a little, happy that someone was interested in talking to him. "We – people from Eastern Europe – grew up with politics. It was our life and our blood. No one knows it better than we do." He coughed a little, but insisted on speaking. "Even here in America, I got a bit involved in local politics and went to some meetings."

However, they had to keep this visit brief because Albert was so weak. Maria exchanged a little news with her brother and then went to talk to his doctor. Nick suggested he wait for her downstairs in the car.

Doctor couldn't tell her anything very reassuring. He said that the operation had just confirmed his earlier diagnosis of terminal cancer. They were awaiting the end any day now. Maria had braced herself for this fateful verdict but it still pained her deeply to have it pronounced out loud.

Maria returned briefly to Albert's room, knowing that his days were numbered. She sat next to him, gave him a big hug and rested her head on his shoulder.

"I couldn't understand who that fellow Nick is," Albert said searching for clarity. "Just how is he connected to Alana? All I could figure out was that he had his eye on you, dolly, the whole time."

"It's not true. You must be teasing me, Albert," Maria looked up startled and soundly denied his observation. "After all, Nick is thirty-five. I'm seven years older than his mother was. It's totally impossible!"

"You know, dolly, when people have one foot in the grave, they can see things more clearly. I saw his face and how his eyes followed you. I'm not a boy, and I can certainly read a man's face. Believe me, that guy's crazy about you."

"But I'm just an old woman!" Maria exclaimed in disbelief.

"You don't look as old as you are. Besides, it's the 'Older Woman' with her mature sexuality that draws the young ones. You're really very attractive, you know."

"Oh, you're just saying that because you're my brother. Maybe you want me to find a man, too, like Alana."

"That's not what I'm saying, dolly," Albert said seriously. "You're the one that this Nick is interested in and you'll have to face it."

Maria was disturbed by this revelation and so agitated that she wanted to avoid meeting Nick and having him drive her home. She left Albert so he could rest and went down to the hospital lobby, sank into an armchair and buried her face in her hands.

She sensed that what Albert had just told her was the truth, and this made her tense and annoyed. Maria had noticed something during their lunch together - a hidden message in Nick's glances, but she had brushed them off as meaningless. She just couldn't accept in her mind and heart that it might be true that Nick was infatuated with her, of all people, and tried to shut out the very thought.

Unwillingly, her mind kept returning to Nick. Maria had to admit that he was a special person: smart, talented, kind, understanding and generous. Add to that fact that he was both handsome and rich – almost like a movie star! Well, that was absolutely not for her, one hundred percent out of the question. And just as she'd supposed, he wasn't even for her dear Alana. He was clearly too high for them both, someone who deserved a kind of super girl, the opposite of herself – a poor, old, unhappy immigrant caretaker.

Why am I even thinking about the remote possibility that he could be attracted to me? Maria thought, being afraid to entertain the feelings and possibilities that were bombarding her brain. No, it's absolutely ridiculous!

After all, Nick came to our apartment looking for Alana. He bought her a fancy new car. He certainly slept with her. So, he might be in love with her. Jesus, I am her mother! I have no right to even think about him in any other way than as a friend and maybe as a future son-in-law. Help me, oh God! I couldn't hurt Alana! I'll never, ever accept anything that could interfere with her happiness.

Nick was surely 'forbidden fruit' and Maria knew that she should suppress any magnetic pull she felt toward him. She must forget his burning and yet tender looks forever. Maybe there was nothing to this idea. It was all a frustrating fantasy or perhaps her sick imagination. Maybe he was just a natural tease and flirt and he was merely playing with her feelings? Maybe it was a silly joke – like the first glass of cranberry juice?

Maria felt feverish. If Albert had noticed, it couldn't be her imagination, only. Nick made no attempt to hide his feelings, and expressed his affection for her openly. Why? He had no right to do that. She had done nothing to encourage him; quite the opposite, in fact. She had always brought up the subject of Alana and had not responded to Nick's forwardness.

Anyway, if the messages Nick sent to her with his eyes were sincere, what should she do about it? For her, such likelihood was an impossible sweet dream, floating far off in the sky. To even hold such a dream in her hands was unbearable and would surely burn her fingers, so she flung it away to the farthest star.

Maria was tired of sufferings, tired of having her dreams dashed. She'd had more than enough pain for one lifetime. Why to harrow herself over nothing? She was scared to reawaken her dormant heart, lying there quietly and calmly after many years of torment and struggle. It was comfortable to have all your love stories in the memory bank, to give you peace in your old age. Maria could admit that to herself and it brought her some measure of reconciliation.

All her passions were now poured into her paintings. They were her babies, the very breath of her soul. Nick, more than anyone, seemed to be able to grasp them, somehow. She didn't quite know how she knew this, but she saw it – he was aroused and excited by the images and emotion on her canvases. Being near the paintings turned him on and attracted him to her; without realizing it, she now understood that she had unconsciously answered his overtures, flirting and teasing back.

It's impossible not to like him, Maria thought. He is so special that every woman in the world would easily fall in love with him. But I am not a schoolgirl. I must have the will power to cut off these feelings.

She had tried her best to be official and cool to him the evening before but she found his charm could even melt an iceberg. Why was Nick so assertive with her today? Only because she objected? Or he was unable to stop himself, either. All these agonizing doubts made her tremble over the muddle she was in.

A great torrent of feelings overwhelmed her like a dam breaking and she was both flustered and frightened by them. Maria felt the seething current of intense impressions had swept her and Nick off their feet and carried them quickly downstream toward the cascading falls. There was nothing she could do to fight the undertow pulling them both downward. It was too late for that. Still, she didn't want to face it and accused herself of letting his attractiveness break down her defenses.

It's only the beginning of these feelings for me, she tried to convince herself. It's still possible to apply the breaks, to cut the knot. It would already be painful, but would avoid certain tragedy later on. If I let these feelings grow, it'll mean a disaster. I must do something drastic now to push Nick out of my life forever.

Still sitting in the busy lobby, but wrapped up in her own torment, Maria reckoned for the next half hour what she should do. She decided not to return to the car, but to run away from the hospital through another exit and let Nick wait for her for one, two or three hours. She was sure that Nick would finally go up and ask Albert when she left, and when he found out it was long ago, would be angry and offended. He would blame and hate her. Everything would be finished and any future relationship killed in the bud.

It was especially hard for Maria to be mean and rude, but she felt she had no other choice. It must be done.

She stood up and slowly walked through the long corridor to the west gate of the hospital. It was on the far side of the block and an unfamiliar street to Maria. She began looking for a bus stop but couldn't find one and asked some young people who were smoking on the corner where she could catch a bus.

"You took a wrong exit," someone answered. "The bus stop is next to the main parking lot, at the front entrance."

Maria thanked them and returned to the lobby, her heart thumping. Now, it had been about two hours since Nick had gone down to wait for her. She was convinced he would already have gone, insulted by her behavior.

Maria entered the hospital cafeteria, bought a cup of coffee and sat at the table, but somehow, couldn't drink. She couldn't even hold the cup because her hands were shaking.

Maybe I'm doing something wrong, she thought in despair. If a mother-in-law is so bad mannered and rude, it could permanently jeopardize his relationship with Alana. I have no right to interfere. However, it's probably better for me to do something like this than to get involved with him. Well, I'm really between a rock and hard place, all right! I feel trapped. There's no solution and no exit for me. Oh, God, please help me! But it's already too late to reconsider what to do. It's all done.

Maria was completely lost and guilt-ridden. She folded her arms on the table, lowered her aching head on them and rested motionless for a time. The next thing she knew, a kindly waitress tapped her on the shoulder and told her it was closing time. She wearily left, leaving her cold, undrunk coffee behind.

Being positive that Nick had already left, Maria ambled around the parking lot toward the bus stop. She unconsciously looked at the remaining cars, feeling frustrated and tired. Without warning, she saw Nick's silver Mercedes in the spot he had parked earlier and her heart sunk.

Oh, gosh, is he still here? Maria thought mortified, feeling like a naughty child caught in the act of sneaking somewhere. Maybe he's waiting inside the building for me and I missed him? How could I ever think of being so rude when he was so nice to bring me here? Then again, maybe it's just a car that looks like his...

Her curiosity got the better of her and she nervously crept up to the driver's window and stopped. Even in the shadow she couldn't believe what she saw.

Nick was there, peacefully sleeping, with his head balanced on his headrest. There was such a serene expression on his face. While his right hand rested on the seat beside him, his left arm was crooked in the open window. The horrible wrist scars he bore were visible, looking pink and raw. Though two months had passed since his suicide attempt, there was a present and scary reminder of the depths he had recently sunk to.

Maria was moved to pity him and reproach herself. She was choked up with emotion and her heart raced.

He had tried to end his life because his best friend had betrayed him, she reminded herself. So, how could I now turn my back to him? Deliver another slap in the face? What for? It would be so cruel and unnecessary. Why? He is as clean and innocent as a child! He wouldn't hurt anyone. He's a special and spiritual man. He doesn't deserve to be treated badly.

Her eyes misted with tears. For a long time, Maria stood near him and watched him sleep. She bit her lips to muffle her sobs, afraid to wake him.

She had no idea what time it was. Out of the blue, the driver of the next car arrived and slammed the door when he got in. Nick quivered, half-opened his lids and blinked sleepily. His mind was not yet awake and he didn't fully understood where he was. When he saw Maria at his window, he broke into boyish grin.

"Sorry," he apologized. "I guess I slept a bit."

She nodded.

"I'm really tired. I didn't sleep at all last night."

"Why?"

"The truth? I was too excited about your paintings…and about you. I was filled with new sensations and far too worked up to get any rest. What time is it now?" he glanced at his car clock. "Oh, it's already six-thirty. Rush hour's almost over. Well, why are you standing there, Maria? Get in and sit down. You know, I'm hungry again. Let's go have dinner somewhere."

Maria went round the car and slid in beside him, obediently, without a word. Her throat was dry and seemed to squeeze out any words she might try to speak.

How stupid my ideas of resistance were, she thought. It's impossible to resist things which are decided by Fate. Sorry, sorry a million times, my dear one. I will never betray you.

Nick looked attentively at her.

"Were you crying?" he asked and tenderly wiped a tear from her chin. "Something about Albert?"

She nodded.

"I know. It's difficult to lose someone," Nick said, offering sympathy. "I remember when my mom was dying. I was sure that I would die with her. But we have to survive. We really do." He paused reflectively. "I know it's possibly funny for you to hear me say that when you see these…"

Nick laughed as he turned his wrists for her to see. "You see, all gone. I'm really feeling much better now. I feel in my bones that something very interesting is going happen in my life. At least I hope so…

How did Albert call you? Little dolly? Hmmm…it's cute. I like it. Smile please, little dolly, we are going out to dinner! We are going to celebrate!"

"Celebrate what?" Maria asked. He was certainly full of romantic surprises.

"Our very first mini-anniversary. We have now know each other for twenty-four hours and … 'this could be the start of something big'," he began singing as he started the engine and pulled out of the hospital lot.

Chapter 8

MARIA CAME HOME LATE FROM dinner bearing a huge bouquet of coral roses. As she entered the kitchen she took in the scene. The table was still decorated for the lunch with Nick.

"My gosh!" she exclaimed.

She had completely forgotten about it and now Alana might arrive at any moment. What could she say to explain it? The truth? It would sound very plausible. Then, should she make something up? No way. Maria never lied to her daughter.

Heavens! Think of something – fast! Maria thought.

She put the roses down on the counter, raced to the storage room to find a spare cardboard box and returned to the kitchen. Hurriedly, she wrapped the silver and china up in tissue paper and packed them in the box, along with the candles and tablecloth.

By the time Alana came home at midnight, everything was neatly stored away out of sight and the regular plastic green tablecloth was back on the table. The full bouquet of roses stood in the middle in a clay jar.

"Wow!" Alana said, suitably impressed when she saw them. "Are they yours or mine, Mom?"

"Mine." It was not easy to find a way to tell the truth.

"Who gave them to you?" Alana wanted to know.

"A man."

"Is that so? Do you have a secret admirer, Mom? That's awesome."

"Well, you advised me to find myself a man."

"I remember. Good for you, Mom. Ro-o-oses!" Alana leaned over and soaked up the fragrance. "They are just gorgeous! Seniors tend to be more attentive and generous. Nick only bought me half dozen tulips."

"He bought you the car," Maria reminded her, feeling very uncomfortable. She wished the earth would swallow her up.

"I know. I'm just talking about flowers. Are you in love with this man, Mom?"

"I don't know," Maria replied, shrugging her shoulders. "We just had our first dinner together."

"But he is in love, for sure. I can tell you," Alana said as she laughed and then kissed Maria's cheek. "Congratulations! Where did you meet him?"

"Here, in this building."

"Oh, is he that lame senior from the twelfth floor? Is his name Stan? I remember he was always around when you were working. What does he do?"

"I don't know, exactly. He owns some kind of business."

"Is he retired?"

"Possibly. I really don't know."

"What did you do during your dinner, if you don't know anything about him?" Alana teased her mother. "Did you eat in silence?"

"No, we had a lot to talk about. Mostly about abstract ideas. About art...about life...about people's feelings."

"Well, I wouldn't have expected it of someone like Stan. Well, anyway, I'm very happy for you, Mom. Do you think you might marry him?"

"No." Maria emphatically stressed. "Never. Forget it. I don't want to talk about it, okay?"

"Ahaaa," Alana laughed, amused by Maria's predicament. "Now you are in my shoes. Do you remember you lectured me when I spent the night with Nick that first time? Now you know how it felt. Sorry, I didn't mean to get back at you when I suggested you find yourself a man. I'm only very curious about these beautiful roses. That's all. Let's just be friends. Do you forgive me? I really have to get to sleep now. Good night."

She yawned, stretched her arms and headed for her room, but paused halfway and returned. "Oh, by the way, have you heard anything more from Nick?"

"He came by this morning, right off after you left. About nine-thirty."

"Did you tell him I'd just gone?"

"Of course."

"And..."

"He said he'll come again."

Alana laughed, "You see, it's working. Well, I'll probably call him in a few days. Night."

Maria suddenly felt very weary. She turned out the kitchen light and went to her bedroom. She lay on her bed, closed her eyes and shuddered. It was all too terrible! What an impossible mess she'd gotten herself in! How would she ever live with it...?

The following morning at ten sharp, Nick arrived on Maria's doorstep. He was loaded down this time with canvases, paints, brushes, and other artist trappings.

Last night at dinner they had agreed that Maria would teach him to paint. He insisted that he really wanted to try and see if he had any talent in that direction. Nick was so inspired by her ability to use paint and color to express her soul that he thought she'd be a good teacher. She had reluctantly agreed after all his entreaties to give him a chance.

Maria admitted him to the apartment and brought a glass of cranberry juice for him. Then they sat on the couch. She hadn't slept well last night and the strain of this encounter was reflected in both her face and body. In fact, she didn't even know how to begin to share what was in her heart, so she reminded silent. Nick easily figured out that something was disturbing her.

"You look so tense and worried today," he observed, expressing concern. "Is it about Albert?"

She shook her head and dropped her eyes. All the while her fingers nervously tortured the hem of her T-short. Nick placed his hand over hers to still them.

"I guess…" he ventured, forcing her to look into his eyes.

"Yes," Maria nodded. "It's about Alana."

"What about Alana?"

"I am her mother and I want to know…"

"Oh, *that's why* you want to know," Nick mocked her sarcastically.

"Yes, *that's why*. I want to know what your relationship with her is."

"That's simple. None."

Maria was braced for a long explanation and his curtness caught her off guard. It baffled her.

"But…" she whispered uncertainly, "…you came to see her two days ago. It must have meant you had something important to tell her."

"That's right," he explained. "I wanted to tell her that everything was over and that I planned to leave the country. That was my message."

"However, Nick, I can see that you are still here in Minneapolis…"

"Well, now the situation has changed."

"And…?"

"Maria, please," Nick looked at her seriously. "You're not a twenty-year-old. You surely know that men hate discussing this kind of things. Besides, I'm not supposed to tell a woman about my involvement with other woman. I just told you that it is finished. That's enough."

"In this situation, let me remind you, Nick. I'm not *another woman*," she retorted. "I'm the mother."

"You *are* a woman. And you know that."

Nick stood up, abruptly, and headed to his bag. Maria watched him, all trembling. She was sure that she did hurt him and he would go away. But he just opened the bag, took out an album, put it on the easel and turned to her.

"Come over here," he fervently requested. "Show me how you hate me now. Teach me how to express those sentiments on canvas. I want to portray the feelings I have for you. I want the paint to take over all that's inside me. Let this be our first and last quarrel forever."

Maria stood and approached him tentatively. Her face was pale.

"Well," she whispered, stammering, "...you just close... your eyes...and try to imagine what color you feel. What colors...do you see?"

Nick put his hand tenderly on her shoulder, pulled her to him and, without warning, kissed her lips. There was nothing more to say.

Am I crazy? What am I doing? These questions quickly flashed through Maria's mind and dispersed. In an instant it was emptied of all thoughts and a fountain of emotions filled the void.

Nick embraced his new love and slowly covered her willing face with gentle kisses, breathing heavily and sliding his warm lips over the surface. Unconsciously, she arched her neck back to receive his expressions of love and he moved down from her cheeks and chin to her throat. Maria was amazed at his impassioned, yet affectionate lovemaking. He was certainly no novice.

Deep inside her awoke a long dormant molten desire, and like a volcano preparing to erupt it set her trembling. Maria had almost completely forgotten what it felt like to experience a man's hands caressing her body. To renew that old sensation was incredible. She found herself surrendering totally to the force.

She endured her pleasure as a long, drawn-out torture; delight dressed in unbearable agony. Her senses were intensely alive, sharp and piercing, but also sweet beyond measure. Maria moaned in ecstasy in Nick's capable hands. She had no power of resistance or response. She drowned in her enjoyment as an object of desire. Her yielding spurred Nick on in his growing excitement as he explored the body and soul in his arms.

Together they completely lost their heads and their self-control. There was no thought or time to undress or move toward a bed. They couldn't even break away from one another in their mutual ardor. Nick deftly lowered Maria onto the rug where they stood – in the middle of the living room – and carefully took hold of her back and hips as if she were made of fragile porcelain.

It was clear that she was a bit awkward because it had passed decades since she had been with a man, so Nick approached her sensitively. The last thing he wanted to do was to scare her or push her away.

Maria opened to him and with each of his movements her pleasure grew. She learned to relax and trust him. Slowly at first he stimulated her and then increased his thrust and speed. At the sensational climax, Maria shook with chills and cramps of orgasm as he came. Then, with her eyes closed, she threw her head back, arched her back and curled into a convulsion, sobbing hysterically.

Nick couldn't tell if she was crying or laughing; he just sank, enraptured with her. Astonished by the strength of her experience he reveled in sharing the moment and wished that it would go on forever.

Nick felt that she was absolutely amazing, truly the woman of his dreams. The wave of enormous power shook her for an extended period, but he wished it could have been longer. He was magnetically drawn to her and unable to pull away. When the surge finally creased, they both collapsed, weak and speechless.

They lay motionless on the rug in their crumpled state and regained a degree of composure. Nick propped himself up on his side, gazing attentively at Maria's placid face. She reclined parallel to him, limp and lifeless. Her lips were parted and quivered with each breath. She was like a dying swan: weak, pure and sacred.

Her blonde bangs, wet with sweat, were matted to her forehead. Nick lovingly touched them with his forefinger. Maria opened her eyes and he had never seen them so deep and wide before. In their vulnerability and delicacy he swore he had never seen anything more beautiful. His confidence and pride expanded: this woman belonged to him, depended on him for her very happiness. Everything had been given freely to him, and he gracefully took it. They were bound together by these unspoken messages.

With his soul calmed and at ease, Nick could have stayed in this position forever, gazing at his beloved. Following this tension and release, the wrinkles under Maria's eyes become more pronounced. He leaned over and kissed them lightly with joy. He knew he had been especially blessed to have found and won this woman.

"Well, what color was it?" she whispered her first words since he had lovingly assaulted her.

"Orange...and dark blue...with silver..." he murmured, smiling. "Maybe a little green..."

A sudden strong knock at the door sobered them in a split second. Maria jumped up, straightened out her skirt and pulled her T-shirt down over her breasts.

"Who the hell is that?" Nick asked in hushed tones.

"I don't know. Some of condo owners, I suppose."

"Then don't open it. Stay with me."

"But I should," she said, running to the door and opening it a crack.

Nick rearranged his disheveled clothes, run his fingers through his hair and returned to the couch. "Maria, my dear, sorry to bother you," he could hear the rasping voice of a senior. "I forgot my keys again. Would you mind opening my suite for me?"

"Of course, Mrs. Johns. I'll just get your key. I'll be with you in a second. Okay?"

"Sure, my dear. Thanks."

Maria grabbed a metal key box from the entrance shelf and found the wonted key.

"Here it is, Mrs. Johns," she said, handing it to the diminutive, gray-haired widow. "Would you mind putting it through my mail slot after you've used it?"

"Of course, of course, my dear."

Maria closed the door and returned to Nick in the living room. When she approached the couch, he firmly grasped her hips and pulled her to sit on his lap. She hadn't sat on anyone's lap since she was a girl and it made her feel much younger. She turned to Nick and stroked his head and explored his face with her soft, warm fingers.

They locked eyes and smiled, knowing that something precious had entered their lives. They both wished that the intoxication that they felt and the peace in their hearts could last eternally. It was real happiness – a rare taste of bliss.

A loud metallic thud caused Nick to sit up straight. "What's that?" he demanded.

"Oh, just the old woman returning the key," Maria explained. "I'm used to the sound of it falling through my mail slot."

"Shit! It's annoying," Nick grumbled.

"It's not so bad. As I said, I'm used to it. Well, Nick, I need to take a shower. I'm wet and smelly. How about you?"

Nick had no time to answer, for another strong knock at the door stopped him.

"Who is that now?"

"I don't know, but I'll answer it," she almost floated to the door. After sex, she found she was amazingly light and ready to fly.

"Don't open it," Nick spoke jealously behind her.

"It's my work. I must."

"Hi, Maria," the three workmen greeted her. A strong smell of cigarettes wafted into her apartment as they spoke. "We've come to fix a sundeck on the roof. We need to bring up some wood. Could you put the pads in the elevator for us, please?"

"Why didn't you call yesterday, Doug?" she asked, unhappily. "I could prepare it for you…"

"We didn't have a clue yesterday that we would start here today. You know…"

"Okay, guys. Just wait a bit. I'll do it in ten minutes."

"We'll unload then. Thank you, Maria."

"Who are they?" Nick asked.

"Carpenters." She ran off to the shower, at last.

In a couple of minutes, Nick heard a soft but precise knock on Maria's door.

I'll push them all away, he thought angrily, as he went to answer it.

A man about his age, refined in appearance, stood at the door. He looked at Nick and then looked down. His eyebrows shifted as he broke into an artificial smile.

"Ha-ha-ha," he said playfully. "Could you pass that on to Maria, Sir?" He handed Nick an envelope and disappeared in a wink. Nick took it to the table where he left it for her.

She emerged from the shower in about five minutes, pink and warm and wrapped in a terrycloth robe. Her short wet hair stood up in spikes.

"Some strange man left you a letter," Nick reported unhappily.

Maria glanced at the table and laughed.

"It's a gay from the fourth floor," she clarified matter for him. "He is our treasurer and responsible for the checks. They need to be passed on to the property manager. I'll do it tomorrow. It's your turn to shower now."

When Nick had finished his shower, Maria was on the phone. She winked and smiled at him, waving him to come closer. Then she pressed the speaker button to let him hear the conversation.

"Maria," Nick could hear a man's concerned voice. "It's Joe calling. How are you today? I have a question for you. Do you know that someone is unloading by the back door? Who are they? Who gave them permission to unload there? Go and check them right now. You should stop them, Maria. We expect you to do your job properly."

"I'll do it right now, Joe. Thank you for letting me to know."

"Who is that idiot?" Nick asked as she hung up.

"He's the president of our board. Unfortunately, he's retired and has nothing better to do than to watch security cameras all day long. You'd think he would know what's going on, but he's terribly uninformed. He often calls to pick on me and usually interprets things the wrong way."

"What a stupid job you have!" Nick exclaimed.

"Not really," Maria laughed. "I like it. The people are nice and I like them. It's fun to socialize with them. Don't worry about me, Nick. I'm okay. But now's your chance. You can help me at last."

"Finally," he chuckled. "Help with what?"

"I need help with hanging the pads in the elevator for the workers. Actually I can do it myself, but I'm really not tall enough. I need to use a stepladder. It'll be much faster if you do it."

"Yes," Nick agreed. "Let's go. I'll be happy to do anything faster, 'cause I'm already 'hungry like a wolf.' That was the expression you used yesterday, wasn't it?"

Maria nodded and laughed. She felt flattered that he remembered her words.

"Thank you," she told him happily. "I promise that we can go out for lunch immediately after this little job..."

It was the first time in Maria's whole life that she had no fear of losing the man she was with. In the past, she never felt totally confident that she wouldn't be dumped at some point. She had even experienced that anxiety with Peter. But now with Nick – though he was younger, handsome and rich – she felt calmly assured of his love.

"Why didn't you ask for my phone number?" he demanded to know some weeks later.

"What do I need it for? I know that everyday, at ten in the morning I'll see you standing at my door."

"But, what if something happened to me? Or, if I was too busy? Or what if I didn't show up?"

"Then, I'd wait. I know that you'll come later. Or you'll call me," Maria explained. "I don't understand you, Nick. Is that a problem for you? Do you really want me to call you? Well, I have no time for that. I'm too busy having sex with you."

Nick laughed at her joke. She was amazing at sex, but not only that. He had always dreamt of a lady love that he wanted to pursue, being tired of women who chased him and ran after him. The way Maria used her womanly powers seemed great to him. He appreciated the unusual balance between them and respected her all the more for the special role she commanded. Finally, he found it - an exciting challenge to manage this relationship like he'd ever wanted.

Nick did show up at her door every day now. What Maria didn't know was that he phoned St. Boniface Hospital every morning to be sure that Alana would be working the same hours. The last thing he wanted to do was run into the daughter while he was courting her mother.

And, as soon as Nick appeared, they went to bed. Maria kept her figure and her body was still attractive. There were minor signs of aging, of course, her skin was too soft and hung loose under her arms, but Nick was not distracted by these points. He had seen so many beautiful young bodies in his life, most of them void of any mystery or deep content. What really turned him on was Maria's extreme sensitivity and rich sensuality, something none of his other lovers could come close to matching. Nick's appetite was so focused on the enormous pleasure she was capable of feeling and giving him in return, that the form of her physical body was of little importance.

Nick loved to caress the whole of Maria for hours on end. He studied each cell of her body, and explored every inch with his fingers, lips and tongue. Step-by-step he drove her to madness, to orgasm after orgasm, and lastly to sublime unconsciousness. He enjoyed watching her writhe, sobbing, and breathless with pleasure. Her convulsions of joy were preludes to repeated rounds of lovemaking as he, with barely a pause, reignited her flame again by touching her erotic zones. His deft fingertips knew exactly where and how to work her up slowly to their mutual benefit. The intensity and creativity of their rapture was endless, but still Nick hungered for more. With eager eyes he drank in the gratification that registered in her contractions and in her entranced facial expression.

Just when Maria reached the point of exhaustion, he entered her, his time about to begin. It was not drawn out because he was already half satiated by caressing and pleasuring her. But he knew how to prolong sex, when and how to time himself to stop and then to begin again. Such sustained intimacy was only possible with a wonder woman like this.

Maria was convinced that she wouldn't survive their daily love sessions. She was afraid that she would burn out completely. So much sex was already thought to be difficult at her age. It was really too much, but she would rather die than let Nick know. She continued to offer him everything and as much as he wanted, without saying a word.

Yet, day by day, Maria was surprised that she was feeling stronger, younger and healthier. With all her activity and the introduction of Nick's rich sperm into her system, she happily felt twenty years younger. He had helped revitalize her not just spiritually, but physically as well.

Being in love and well-loved is truly the fountain of youth, she now understand.

Nick insisted on retrieving the elegant lunch décor from the storage room and displaying them daily in her humble kitchen. The touch of beauty added to the simple menus they enjoyed together when they broke for refreshment.

"I want to see these things in use every day, Maria," Nick instructed her firmly. "Don't hide them. We aren't thieves and you have nothing to hide. Anyway, Alana will find out about us one day. It's better if she gets used to the idea, step-by-step."

Maria was thrilled deep down in her heart to learn that Nick was not a boy at all; he was a strong and powerful man with his own opinion and determination. She was so happy that she was not in a "mothering" role; in fact, she was the weaker one, the possessed. At the same time, they were the best of friends, sharing many interests and a deep wordless understanding of each other. They both reveled in their dynamic unity.

Right away, Alana noticed the new table settings as she entered the apartment.

"Wow!" she exclaimed. "A new present from Stan! I heard from the others that he is pretty selfish, but it must be just gossip. I actually remember him bringing us oranges when he returned from visiting his kids in Arizona. Right, Mom?"

"Yes. I remember, too," Maria laughed.

"I'm sure he plans to marry you, Mom. Men usually give women gifts for the house when they want to marry them."

"I don't know," Maria refused to commit herself.

"Why not? Think about it. Anyway, at your age, you probably don't have feelings or love left, but Stan is pretty well off. It could make your life more comfortable."

"Don't be so disgusting, sweetie," Maria objected.

"Sorry, Mom. It was just a joke. To change the subject, how about Nick? Did he come looking for me?"

"No," Maria told her, and it was true. "Actually, I don't know. I'm still spending every evening with Albert at the hospital."

It was also true. Albert was still the most important person in Maria's world. It didn't matter how busy she was or what was happening in her life. He was number one and she stubbornly carried on visiting him nightly and sitting with him for hours, holding his hand. When he was awake and conscious, she did talk to him but mostly he slept under heavy medication. These evenings Maria just hugged him, rested her head on his shoulder and slumbered with him, trying to share the warmth of her heart as a memorable farewell. It was enough for both of them to sense the other's closeness.

However, Albert's life was swiftly nearing its end.

One morning upon arrival Nick found Maria sobbing. She tried not to, but her lips were quivering. She was working at the easel, applying paint to her unfinished image.

"Albert?"

She just nodded.

"When?"

"This morning," she whispered. "The memorial service and funeral will be in two days."

Maria threw her arms around Nick and buried her face on his chest. She allowed herself to let out the grief that had enveloped her. She found it difficult to talk.

"They called me... this morning at six. I won't forgive myself...for not being there...with him. My only brother! I wanted to hold his hand...when he went. It's my fault.

"I was with him every night...until I met you," she lamented, tears streaking her puffy face. "But now I'm so tired, so exhausted. I need to sleep at night. But I was with him yesterday...until midnight. He was quiet and sleepy. There was no pain, thank God. Since he was calm I guessed that he would be all right...for another day. I took a taxi and came home to sleep. He died during the night, but I was sleeping! I missed him! I lost my dear brother! I'm alone in this world now!"

She was helpless like a little girl who had just lost her hero and protector in the world. Nick comfortingly held and rocked her, stroked her hair and kissed her moist eyes. He could empathize with her powerlessness and emptiness, for he had lost his own mother. Maria couldn't stop crying softly and bemoaning her failures.

Finally, Nick touched her chin and looked straight into her blue eyes. "I know you are distraught with the loss of Albert," he said firmly, "but that doesn't give you a right to say foolish nonsense. Of course you are *not* alone in this world. You know that."

"I know that you're there for me," Maria said between sobs. "But he was my brother, my own flesh and blood, and you are only a lover..."

"Am I *only* a lover?" Nick asked upset. "Just a regular lover? Just one of many lovers? You better think about what you are saying!"

Nick pushed her away, stung by her words. He sat on the couch, lips pursed and breathing heavily. His hands had become angry fists of outrage.

"A lover is an accidental person who comes into your life and then goes out. A stranger, in other words," Nick's voice was quavering. "For me, our relationship is on another level. It is too eternal and holy to be so labeled. And I thought it was the same for you, too. Honestly, I'm shocked! I don't want you to say another thing because I don't want to listen to you anymore.

"Please, Maria, just paint. I'll sit quietly and watch. And then I'll decide what to do with you."

It was like a blast of cold water on her hot face. She sobered in a flash, suddenly realizing how deeply she had cut him. She didn't have the courage to turn to him and look at his face. Silently, with shaking wrists, Maria replaced the unfinished canvas with a pristine, new one on the easel. She closed her eyes in meditation and breathed deeply. Then she took up her palette, squeezed out some fresh colors, mixed a few with her palette knife, and faced her feelings. As a new image took form in her soul, she began to transfer it to the surface in front of her, slowly and methodically. Her hand and mind steadied as she became absorbed in the process of creation.

Nick's angry eyes bore into her back, but true to his word, he said nothing. He caught each new brushstroke she applied to the canvas, each new color, each new form. Without hurry, Maria painted and painted, giving of herself to bring it to life. New tears followed the rivulets down her cheeks of the ones for Albert, but she didn't wipe them away.

Nick waited impatiently, but had no clue as to the drama unfolding before him. He had no idea what this new painting would represent, and what meaning it would hold for him.

Then a shock of recognition came to him. There it was…orange… and dark blue…with silver…and hints of green. He remembered it all perfectly. It was their first explosive sexual encounter. It was passion and desire, love and affection, two soul mates sharing their essence. The painting recorded this historic, earth-shaking beginning of their powerful love.

Now Maria had given him the answer he needed. She had done it for him! She truly loved him and was begging for his forgiveness.

Nick had no words to respond to her message. He was stoned from excitement and awed by her talent to communicate something so personal and universal. She wasn't just a talented woman. In truth, she was an artistic genius.

Maria put down her palette and brushes and turned round to Nick. She slowly approached him repentantly. She kneeled in front of him, not daring to look into his eyes. But she could sense that anger was no longer raging in him. She put down her aching head on his lap and rested there, in breathless expectation of her fate. Nick tenderly placed his hand on the nape of her neck.

Feeling doomed, she uttered a quiet and resigned, "I love you, Nick."

"I'll marry you," he announced boldly. "Immediately!"
He rose, lifted her up and carried her to bed.

Chapter 9

ABOUT A MONTH PASSED BEFORE Alana woke up to the fact that her plan for snaring Nick was failing. The friends' advice she had been given was probably wrong, as well. She felt oppressed with despair and frustration. So she was driven back to her old tactics which at least had provided her a chance now and then to see Nick and sleep with him. This illusion of love she carried was one she needed very much, and it was certainly better than nothing. Her passion had grown and she felt she wouldn't be able to live without him. Little of this obsession was visible on the outside so nobody, even her mother, suspected how serious her desperation was.

On top of it all, Alana discovered, with horror, that she was pregnant. She tried her best to deny it, even buying a home pregnancy test to check her suspicions. Of course, the results were positive. Finally she went to consult a doctor.

The doctor confirmed that she was six weeks pregnant. That was perfect timing for her last encounter with Nick in her apartment.

Most of the time, Alana sobbed alone to herself. To have a baby now would certainly mean a dead end to all her dreams. The only solution then would be - an abortion without letting anyone know. She felt she wanted to talk to Nick about it.

At this point, Alana's supervisor at St. Boniface told her one day that a man had been calling every morning and asking about her shift time. That gave her hope. Alana easily guessed that it was Nick. It reassured her that he hadn't lost interest in her and that she might be able to salvage something from this situation.

Alana resumed her driving practice and surveillance of Nick's house and office. He wasn't either place so it brought no results. She called his house and left several messages, but they remained unanswered. When she finally phoned his office, his secretary said that Mr. Bell was away on vacation.

That explains everything, Alana thought. I still have time. It will be up to him whether the baby lives or dies.

She relaxed a little and for a few days was calm. Then, one evening she decided to call his house from her home and was even pleasantly startled when he picked up the phone. On his phone display, Nick saw the *River Valley Condominium* number and assumed that Maria was calling. Instead, and disappointingly, he found himself on the line with Alana.

"Hi, Nick," she said, trying to sound casual about it. "My mom mentioned that you came here a couple of times looking for me."

"Yes, I did," he answered as he took a deep breath. "It was more than a month ago already. You are not an easy person to find."

"Just like you. Why did you want to see me?"

"We were friends, Alana. I did promise to let you know about my decision – how we would continue our relationship. You know, I had lots of problems here. So, I decided to travel for a year or two, very far away, go to South America. I can't continue working in business any longer and I can't stay here anymore. I'll go and you'll remain. So we'll just part, stay friends, and send each other Christmas cards. That's all I can tell you."

"But I can't live without you, Nick," Alana admitted, biting her lips and trying not to cry. "I love you."

"I know, Alana. It must be difficult for you, and I'm very sorry to hurt you. Believe me, I never wanted that. I didn't encourage you to fall in love with me. It just happened. I really appreciate it, but I don't feel the same way."

"That's cruel!" she exclaimed. "That's not fair!"

"Alana, please! You must understand me. Just relax and try to forget everything between us. You have your whole life before you. You'll find the perfect man, I promise you."

"I don't think so. I need to see you badly, Nick. I have something important to tell you, and it shouldn't be over the telephone."

"It won't work, I'm afraid. I'm not going to give you any more false hopes. I told you the truth and now you must accept it. Forgive me if I did anything wrong. Bye."

Nick hung up and when Alana repeatedly tried to ring him back, he refused to answer.

She once more found herself crying in despair, and doubled her resolve not to tell her mother anything. She was absolutely certain what Maria would tell her.

I told you this man is not for you. I told you to stick with Tom, but you don't listen to me. Now you know I was right. You should keep your baby and marry Tom...and decide to be happy with him.

Alana had no desire to hear such a lecture. She knew from her friends that all parents were like that – boring, nagging and never wrong. Her brave heroine character was supposed to resolve herself the own situation.

She wanted to catch Nick in person and tell him about their baby. She wanted to see his face, his reaction. He already told her he didn't love her. Well, he would probably love their baby.

Alana continued her driving practice and waited for hours beside Nick's house. She even took some days off work to have more time to spy on him. Then, she finally caught him.

Nick drove out of his garage and headed downtown. Alana followed him, trying to keep her distance and not let him to see or recognize her. But with her flashy red car, so familiar to him, he probably caught sight of her. He suddenly increased his speed and she sped up as well. This 'chase' was not so easy because of quite traffic. Luckily, there were no police around.

Nick increased his speed again, and Alana did, too. She would rather have an accident and die than lose sight of him. Their cars flew along, whizzing and skidding at turns. Pedestrians dashed aside, scared for their lives. The other drivers braked and cleared the way as best they could. It began to resemble an action movie car chase straight out of Hollywood.

Alana pursued Nick so stubbornly that he felt he couldn't escape and that it would only end when one or both of them had a horrible crush. He should stop it. He must be the smarter and more mature one to put an end to it.

Nick braked abruptly and pulled over. He caught her off guard and her brakes screamed as she tried to stop behind him. She missed ramming his car by only a few inches.

He jumped out of his car and ran to her, angrily. She was shaking as she emerged from her Ford Focus.

"What the hell are you doing?" he exclaimed. "Can't you see how ridiculous and dangerous this is? What do you want from me? This is fucking nuts! You will never get me to love you by doing some fool kid-stunt like that. You're pushing me to hate you instead!"

He glared hard at her, breathing heavily and narrowing his eyes. Alana approached him and put her arms around his neck, hoping to calm him down, but Nick abruptly and forcefully pushed her hands away.

"I don't want to get into an accident because of you. I was nice and polite with you until you made me mad. Please live me alone – forever! I don't want to see you again. That's it – it's completely over between us."

Nick looked at her face. He was surprised that he had already forgotten what Alana looked like. She didn't resemble Maria at all. She was completely different – taller and bigger. Her gray eyes were rounded and her brown hair was curly.

Really different features. She must take after her father, Nick reasoned.

He faintly remembered Peter's photo that Maria had shown him once. Now this lack of resemblance to Maria made Alana seem like a complete stranger. She wasn't his woman, or even a friend he knew, anymore.

"I love you, Nick," Alana said, begging him with her eyes. "And I have to tell you I'm pregnant."

He was filled with resentment and found himself laughing at this unexpected news.

"That old trick has been tried on me several times already. Don't play childish games with me."

"But it's true," she said sincerely.

"Well then, why are you telling me this? What do you want from me? Money?"

To Alana this reply was like a slap in the face.

"I hate you!" she shouted in her frustration. "I don't want anything from you! At all!"

"Thank you," he responded, agitated, and returned to his car. He got in, slammed his door and drove away, leaving her with no hope at all.

Alana returned home and cried the whole day, moping around the house. It was the day of Uncle Albert's funeral, so her tears were well-timed. Maria's eyes were not dry either, so she didn't notice anything unusual was going on with her daughter. They shared their tears and hugged at home following the service.

"Tomorrow I'll go to camp with Jessica," Alana told her mother. "I took two weeks off work and I need a brake."

"Are you sure you're okay?" Maria asked her. "You look pale."

"Yes I'm okay. I'm just tired. That's why I need to go somewhere. I need to relax in the sunshine."

Alana took out Tom's engagement ring. She kept it in a jewelry box after Tom left and hadn't worn it. Now she slipped it on her finger.

"If Tom calls," she said, "just tell him I love him."

"Sure, sweetie," Maria confirmed and looked at her attentively. It was the last thing she would've expected her to say.

My gosh! Maria thought. Young people are so hard to understand sometimes. Alana is always jumping here and there. She's only a child and filled with confusing feelings and impulses. She's hardly a girl who is serious about her relationship with men.

Nick didn't appear for three days following the funeral so Maria had some extra time to do the things at home she'd been neglecting recently. She did a very big laundry, deeply cleaned her suite, and cooked some good meals ahead. The past month had been a trying and tiring one with Albert's last days, her work and these daily trysts with Nick. Now, she could breathe deeply and relax a little. At last she felt inspired to paint again.

Maria missed having Nick around, of course. Every cell of her body called out for him, but her mind knew that he had some good reason for not coming by. She trusted him in full. If he wasn't with her then that meant that he was busy with something and would come later. She believed in him, waiting and painting the unfinished image of her love.

Nick spent his time at home. After the scene with Alana on the street, he returned home angry and turned to his whiskey. He followed that with a long sleep and when he awoke he reflected on what had happened.

Alana really infuriated him. She made things so difficult. Instead of ending like good friends she pushed him into a corner and they turned into enemies. And now here he was drinking again. He certainly didn't want that. He didn't have any idea what he would have to do to get her out of his hair.

Nick was positive of one thing: Maria shouldn't know anything about it. He was sure it would poison their beautiful relationship which had become the most valuable thing in his life. He needed to come up with a solution to this mess.

Other problems were gnawing away at him as well. They all made him nervous and irritated. He had to find some answers soon but he figured he couldn't do it alone.

For three days Nick pined for Maria, not just physically and sexually, but mentally and spiritually, as well. He finally confessed to himself that he couldn't exist without her by his side.

Nick felt that she was what he had been missing his whole life, but, because he hadn't met her sooner, he had no idea that a woman like her was walking the earth somewhere in the world. Now that he knew, he understood that there was no point in living alone. He didn't even want to waste a single minute, so at ten o'clock the following morning he returned to the *River Valley* building.

Maria opened her door.

"I missed you, my love," she shone from happiness at the sight of him. "Cranberry juice?"

"Of course. As usual," he nodded. "I have something for you too."

Drinking the juice, Nick could read some anxiety behind the smile on Maria's face.

"Something about Alana again?" he asked tensely.

"No. She is okay. She's gone for two weeks camping with her friends. I'm just concerned...It's my work. There are a couple of teenagers who are messing things up and making extra work for me. I'm getting really tired of it. Then, the president is also on my case – this is wrong, that's no good, you can clean it better. He's always threatening to fire me..."

"Stop it, little dolly," Nick said, inviting her to sit on the couch.

He sat down and cuddled Maria on his lap. He encircled her waist and felt her presence fill him.

"Look into my eyes, my love," he spoke seriously. "What are we talking about? What building? What president? What crazy owners? What job? You, with your brain, education, talent and soul do not need to serve as a butt for humiliations. Maria, you must not clean the dirt after those people. It's criminal! Do you think I could possibly allow it any longer? No way!"

Just then someone knocked on her door. Maria stirred to answer it, but Nick held her tight.

"You are not going to respond," he said sternly.

"But I should."

"I said no. You are not working here anymore. I already called *West-Build* and told them that you're to be fired."

"My goodness! How will I live?" Maria gasped.

"You'll live in my house because I've got a better job for you. You're going to become my wife."

Nick then proceeded to take a small jewelry box from his pocket.

"Do you know what this is?"

"A ring?" she whispered not quite believing what she saw. "Nick, don't you think I'm a little old to be your Cinderella?"

"You are just what I need," he answered, kissing the new fallen tears from her cheeks. He took out the ring. "Give me your finger, little dolly."

"Five diamonds!" Maria remarked in amazement. "Are you crazy, Nick? I don't deserve this."

"You deserve much more, Maria. You deserve all my love and all my life. I can't even say how it happened. It's a big mystery, that's all I know."

Nick gently placed the ring on her finger and gave her a full-blown kiss.

"One problem is solved," he whispered. "Now let go to bed and solve another one..."

Three hours later, they were lying in bed in one another's arms, happy and completely satisfied. They sought out each other's eyes and smiled.

"Now the second problem is solved," Nick said quietly. "We still have a bunch more. Shall we discuss them now?"

"Why not?" Maria snuggled up on his chest. "If I can help you with something…"

"We should leave on our honeymoon soon. But it won't be just for a few weeks, it should go on longer. Maybe even a year or more…I have no clue where to. I thought about South America, but I'm not sure that's best. Can you suggest somewhere?"

"Germany?" she proposed. "I haven't been there for almost twenty-three years."

"Really? That's great idea! It's amazing, Maria. You are truly my angel."

"Haven't you ever been there?"

"No. As a student I traveled every simmer with Gary and other friends. We went to Europe many times: France – Paris and the southern coast, Spain, Italy, Portugal, then north to Holland and Sweden. But we never visited Germany."

"You have seen so much more than me. I've only traveled to the Eastern European countries, as a journalist."

"Now you can make up for lost time, then. But we'll start with Germany. It's perfect. Thank you, my little dolly."

"Oh, and I have a request," Maria continued shyly. "If you really love me…"

"That's not a question."

"…and you really want to marry me…"

"That's not a question, either."

"…could we have the wedding in West Berlin?"

"But, Maria, there's no West Berlin anymore. It's just Berlin now."

"Well… in Berlin then. At St. Peter's Cathedral? Father Jorgen could marry us in my blue glass refuge, the place where I hid. It would be holy and symbolic for me to begin my new life there."

"Is Father Jorgen still alive?"

"Yes, he's eighty-three now. He's retired but sometimes he still conduct services in his church. We exchange cards with him every Christmas and Easter."

"You are so wise, my love," Nick observed and covered her in kisses once more. "Your ideas are great. One more problem easily solved!"

"I'm just wondering, Nick. Can you really leave your office for so long? Will your father agree to such a leave-of-absence?"

Nick took a deep breath and looked at her.

"Another problem remains that I can't seem to resolve," he said. "My business. I hate it. My father pulled me into it when I was an inexperienced child. Now I've overgrown it. I want desperately to leave it, but there are two important reasons why I haven't already. One – I don't know what to replace it with, and two – I can't hurt my father."

Maria studied his face, her own filled with amazement.

"I can't really understand what you're saying, Nick. What do you mean? You don't know what to do? With what?"

"With myself. I'm still young and full of energy. I'm capable of doing something useful in my life. I don't want to be a rich playboy type, filling my life with only eating, sleeping, traveling and having sex. I want to do something significant. I tried to learn to paint from you, but, as you can see, I'm not very good. I don't have your special talent. I don't know what else to try…"

"Nick, are you kidding me?" Maria wanted to know.

"Absolutely not. I'm at loose ends."

"You must be kidding me. You couldn't be so blind as to miss your great talent. Nick, you are a writer! You are already a talented and successful writer. Can't you see it?"

"Me?"

"Yes, you! You already wrote a best-selling book. And it was just your first. It's recognized as a gifted book. One of the best, if I remember correctly. Anyway, you are a writer and an outstanding one at that!"

Nick reacted with a bitter smirk.

"Oh, that. It was just my treatment. I loved doing it, but I never took it seriously. Then it was stolen from me. Gary is the 'writer' now. It's too painful and I don't want to discuss it, dolly."

"You should, Nick." Maria counseled him as she sat down on the bed. She was excited and couldn't fathom why he couldn't see something so obvious to everyone else. "Listen to me, please," she said worriedly. "I'll try to explain it to you. At first writing was just an experiment. You don't consider it successful because it was stolen from you. But, at the same time, it *was* successful because it gave you the possibility to discover your great talent. You can see what you are capable of, what you can accomplish. Gary stole your book – true. But he is dull and ungifted and will never write another book. In fact, he will choke on your book."

"You suffered a lot, but still you survived. It's over. Forget Gary and your first book. Who needs them? But don't forget your talent for writing. That's what the book showed the world. You must write another book, then one more, then another… You owe it to yourself. You must correct this wrong. Yes, I'm sure it will be more difficult. You'll start from zero as a writer because of Gary's betrayal. But you can do it. I believe in you.

"Today, it may look like Gary is the winner, but in reality, he will lose everything. You'll see. You'll easily surpass him, if you continue writing. I know that. I feel it in my bones. I'm sure because I know you are a gifted person, Nick."

Maria was overflowing with love and passion for this man. Her eyes were sparkling with faith in him.

"I love you, Nick, and I'm absolutely sure that writing is your real calling. I promise to be with you forever; I'll help you as much as I'm able to. Remember, I was a journalist. And, as an artist, I can illustrate your books. I'll give your advice whenever you ask for it..."

"...and satisfy me with lots of sex," he laughed. "Don't feel offended, dolly. I'm not teasing you. Seriously, when I was writing my first book I went without sex. After Laura, I gave up on women for awhile. The young, long-legged Barbie-beauties nauseated me and filled me with disgust. I always imagined them making love to cats or dogs.

"Obviously the shock cut me too deeply. Really deeply. All the day long I was preoccupied with business affairs. I returned home only to write every evening. Maybe I become a little crazy because of that. It was not normal. I missed sex during my most powerful years – my mid-thirties – and my mind was twisted. That's probably why I'm insatiable now and can't get enough sex. I even want you more and more every minute. I didn't want to discuss it before, but there's no reason now to hide things from you. I want you to understand where I'm coming from."

"I do, my love. I went without sex for many years, too, don't forget. I was convinced that I would never experience it again. Maybe that feeling unconsciously pushed me to express myself through painting. I don't know. I'm just guessing. But I do know that we're happy together. So, why not to create another book?

"I know that for creative work you need to suffer," Maria continued. "It's the same as a plant that needs soil for its roots. Otherwise you cannot succeed. But the past year has given you plenty of fertile soil for future books..."

"Okay. Do you have any idea what my next book should be about?"

"A story about Gary stealing your book? A story about your suicide attempt? A story of Alana's revenge on Gary? My German story? Or...our love story? There are so many ideas that spring to mind. All you have to do is put them down and shape them."

Nick gave a thoughtful look out the window.

"I don't know," he said uncertainly. "I never thought about it. Are you suggesting that I go back over all the pain in my soul? Open up my wounds? I don't want that."

"Maybe it sounds strange to you, Nick, but we need it for both of us. It's like salt, pepper and other seasonings in cooking. If we only have incredible sex all the time, things will soon get pretty insipid. I'm afraid our love will slip away. But if together we had a mutual connection based spiritually on our creative output that would bind us together for eternity. Believe me. I already had something like that with Peter.

"Other love relationships I had that lacked the spiritual connection were short-lived and scattered like ash in a breeze. Can't you see that the same thing happened with your previous lovers – a shallow and unsustainable affinity? I love you too much, Nick, and I want this love between us to grow and last. I'm sure you don't want to lose me, either. So, I propose that you start your second book. Think about it first; then sit down to write."

Nick looked at her with admiration.

"I never thought that the mind of a woman would arouse me so much," he laughed. "Or am I the only man in the world deserving of such wisdom? I'm not joking, little dolly. You are so clever that I'm ready to kneel at your feet and kiss you hands in adoration. You are exactly the person I've been looking for my whole life. And I couldn't find you until now."

"You needed a woman with a mind. Not every man needs that. Many men would rather not know if their woman can think or not. They don't care."

"I used to be one who didn't care," Nick admitted, "with Laura, and most other girls, believe me. That's why I crashed. It's probably why I tried to take my life. I needed a strong, thinking woman beside me when the mess with Gary and the book happened. There was no one to protect me and advise me, no one to inspire me to go forward. I'm agreeing with you, my love. I don't know what my new book will be about but I'll do it – for us. Thank you, my little dolly."

He passionately planted a kiss on her face.

"Stop, stop, stop it!" she insisted, moving away from him and blocking his lips with her palm. "Stop it now, otherwise in a minute we won't stop. We're not finished talking yet."

She gave him a big, reassuring smile and asked, "Have you chosen what to do with your life now, Nick? Have we solved the question about your business, as well?"

"Not completely. There is one more, important matter. I can leave business for writing, but I don't know how to break it to my father. The news would just destroy him. He's invested so much in me. He's dreamt of out partnership his whole life. If I left now, I'd be betraying his hopes. For me this is a really big problem and there isn't any solution, I'm afraid."

Maria thought a bit, biting her lower lip and tracing imaginary pictures on the sheet with her index finger.

"Well," she said, "do you want me to speak to him for you?"

"You?" he asked, a little startled.

"Yes, me. Anyway, you have to introduce me to him somehow – or not?" her voice quavered. "Or are you ashamed to say that you will be married to an old immigrant caretaker?"

"Maria, stop putting yourself down like that. You are not a caretaker anymore...and in reality you never were."

"I was, too. And I still am an immigrant. And I am an old woman, next to you!" she exclaimed, heatedly.

"Stop it! I asked you not to say that!" Nick's eyes flared. "I'll never allow anyone to say that about you – even you. Why are you trying to hurt my feelings like that?"

"Because you hurt mine. What did you mean by *You?* Do you think I'm not capable of talking to your father?"

"I didn't say that. I was just surprised, that's all. I'd never thought about it. I was only thinking about how to win you over, and then – how completely you fill me up. I just didn't connect my love for you to my father. That's another world. That's why I'm surprised. We need to come up with a solution rather than attacking one another like this."

Nick saw by her defiant reaction how deeply and sharply she had suffered through her immigrant experience in America; how painful it had been for her to live and work far below her capabilities. He realized how much humiliation she had undergone and digested because she didn't have a resentful soul. Her triumph over suffering made her holy in his eyes.

Nick took her hands between his and kissed them.

"I'm sorry, Maria. So sorry, my love," he whispered, "on behalf of all of America – for all the humiliations you've had here. I'll take you to your castle, my Cinderella. You'll have all that you deserve. I promise."

"I'm sorry, Nick," Maria returned with her own apology. "I'm so silly sometimes, and am full of too much pride. I shouldn't be like that with you."

"Forget it, dolly. We've already forgiven one another. Well, I've got a good idea for you, now. But I need to make a couple of phone calls right away."

In about an hour a professional photographer buzzed Maria's apartment. Nick knew him because he often worked for the Bells. With a quality camera and loaded with lighting equipment, he proceeded to take pictures of Maria's paintings from different angles. Two hours later, Nick and Maria examined a table full of pictures, trying to select the twenty best. They drove the selected ones to the printers the Bells also used.

In two days, ten slick photo albums of Maria's artwork were produced, beautifully designed, using the highest quality of glossy paper.

The cover read: Maria Bell, Paintings.

"You are a magician," Maria enthused as she viewed the stylish results. Her tears began as she gave Nick a grateful hug.

"No, no, no. Calm down," he instructed, patting her back. "It's okay. Please don't feel indebted. I'm actually pretty selfish. I really did this for myself. I need it even more than you now, believe me."

Right away that the album was ready, Nick made an appointment with Gustav Bell.

"Dad," he told him, "I want you to meet the woman I love."

"Oh," Gustav Bell laughed. "Is she the brave sweetheart who spit in Gary's face for you, in front of all of America?"

"No, Dad. I'm sorry. She's a foreign journalist and a pretty famous artist, as well."

"That's a new direction for you," the elder Bell commented. "You keep coming up with surprises. I hope this will be a pleasant surprise, at last."

"It will be – she is already my wife."

"Oh-oh, so fast? I didn't expect that!" Gustav Bell exclaimed.

"Me, neither," admitted Nick.

They made an appointment for the day after tomorrow.

When Nick hung up, Maria declared, "You lied to him."

"No, little dolly. What did I say that isn't true?"

"I am not famous…"

"I'm talking about your future. In my heart you are very famous."

"…and I am not Maria Bell."

"Big deal. You will be right away."

Then, in fifteen minutes they drove to the City Clerk's Office to register their marriage and take blood tests. After waiting 24-hours and getting the results, they would be able to tie the knot.

"And now, my Cinderella, your carriage is waiting," Nick told her. "Let's go and buy a special dress."

"Thank you, I have enough already."

"I'm sure you do, little dolly, but to meet my father you should wear a thing that will knock his socks off! I know his taste – classy and expensive."

They parked outside the Paris in America shop to choose something extra special. Maria tried on several possibilities. Finally together they decided on a deep red English suit and accessorized it with matching heels and purse. A white silk blouse set off her neckline, and pearl earrings and necklace framed her face. Nick selected a lovely, delicate gold watch as a wedding present and had it engraved.

Maria then modestly asked, if she could buy a bottle of Christian Dior's Lily of the Valley perfume.

"My father prefers White Diamond," Nick replied. "Okay, we'll get both of them; one for us and one for visiting him. Okay, my dolly?"

"Okay, if it's not too expensive. I guess your father will block your account after you spend all this money on me."

Nick burst out laughing, almost to tears.

"You are so sweet, dolly," he said, hugging her as he finally stopped to laugh. "Don't worry about me. I have enough accounts."

The next day, they picked up their tests, and were pronounced Mr. and Mrs. Bell in front of two office clerk witnesses. Then, they returned to her suite to toast to their future with some champagne.

Maria took one of her albums and autographed it for Gustav Bell.

Dear Mr. Bell, she wrote. *It's me, Maria. This is my heart and soul. I give it to you sincerely. Look to this album attentively. I hope these paintings will help you to understand your son.*

Then Nick took the other albums to his house for safe-keeping. He was aware that Alana could appear home at any minute.

Maria needed time to practice walking in her new high heels. She hadn't dressed up like this once in the past twenty-five years - then she was a well known reporter approaching members of the government and visiting dignitaries. She had almost forgotten how to walk in heels, but she quite soon got the hang of it. As she walked, she practiced holding her head high and keeping her shoulders straight.

Nick was amused to watch Maria walking and enjoyed a lot, teasing her that she is ready to be in a beauty pageant. They laughed like children and reveled in all these preparations.

When it was time to see Gustav Bell, Nick grew nervous again. They agreed that he should wait in the reception area with the secretary while Maria went to see his father alone. She felt confident enough and was convinced that he wouldn't remember that he saw her last year as a caretaker at *River Valley.*

The elder Bell and Maria pleasantly got to know one another. He asked her some questions about Germany, her work as a journalist and why she had come to the U.S. Maria explained that she was widowed, and came to Minneapolis at an invitation of her businessman brother. Then the topic turned to art, and she put the album lovingly in his hands. Together, they turned the pages and discussed the paintings. Gustav considered that he didn't know much about art, but would be happy to learn from her in the future.

"I'm sorry," he said. "I never had time for the arts. I guess I worked too hard. My wife, Natalie, was crazy about things like art, fine music, poetry and literature. She had pretty special, but tragically short life. She got cancer when Nick was only one year old and struggled through fifteen years of treatment. As much I loved her I couldn't save her. But all those years she and Nick were so close so he got an education in the beautiful things in life."

Then he leaned back in his leather armchair and looked attentively at her face. Maria was sure that he was trying to guess her age. It was obvious that she was older than Nick - but just how much older, he wondered. Maria appreciated the fact that Gustav Bell was discrete enough not to say anything on this subject or show disapproval. He was perceptive and could understand what his son found in this older woman. It was impossible to deny the attractiveness of her mature sexuality and her adroit mind which he grasped from the first minutes of their conversation. He could make no objection to this match. Meanwhile, Maria was squirming under his studied gaze.

"So, why have you come to see me without Nick," he asked warily. "Where is that husband of yours – and son of mine – by the way?"

Now, the spotlight was on her and her ability to mediate between father and son in these dangerous waters. Nick's future happiness depended on it. Maria took a deep breath and plunged in.

"Mr. Bell, I wanted to talk to you in private," she explained, giving him a warm smile. "Nick will be in later. But first I want to make some things clear to you. So..."

She hesitated for a moment, hoping the atmosphere was warm enough to handle the news she would deliver. "You love Nick. And I love him, too. We both love him, don't we? Of course, we love him in different ways, but both of us want him to be happy at long last. Isn't that true?"

Gustav Bell nodded although he couldn't imagine what she was getting at.

"Are you happy, Mr. Bell, with your work? I mean do you *like* business?"

"That's a strange question," he objected. "I can't say if I like it or not. It's my life. Can you say you like breathing? Not really. It's just a big part of your life. You have to do it, otherwise you'll die. Same thing with..."

"I know you always dreamt that it would be Nick's life, as well. You did everything possible to make that happen and you expected that it would. He was always a good son and followed your directions. Well, he is still a good son, but you can't imagine how much he suffers trying to please you."

"Really?" Gustav Bell knitted his brows in surprise. "He is actually quite spoiled, I think."

"I'm sorry, but I see Nick from different perspective. He has a sensitive soul and a depth that he's been unable to express. In addition, he is gifted by fate...or by God, if you prefer another word. For most men being put on the road to a successful business career would be just the ticket. It would be many men's greatest dream. Nick thought it was for him, too, but he can see now how little he understood himself. After all, he was just an adolescent when you laid out his future for him.

"Now, Nick realizes that he has no calling to the business world. But he will go to great lengths not to offend you. This dilemma has already taken him to the edge of existence, and it might return him there again – if he doesn't have the chance to discover and use his own gift. He simply needs to do what he was put into this world to do."

"What do you mean by 'gifted'?" Gustav Bell asked thoughtfully, still knitting his brows.

"I mean his writing talent."

"But that damn book was exactly why he wanted to kill himself! It was just his..." The word *stupidity* almost slipped out but he caught himself and substituted another word, "...naivety to get mixed up with this canning..." Again Gustav avoided his first choice of terms, *bastard,* "...insidious 'friend'. What are you suggesting? To set the same thing in motion again? To push him to another suicide? To finally lose my son?"

"The last thing I want to do is to upset you, Mr. Bell," Maria apologized. "I'm sorry if it looks like I'm interfering in family matters. All I'm asking for is a chance to keep Nick happy and healthy. That's all. And I can see that his profound unhappiness over the family business could threaten his life. He's looking for a way to escape what he dreads, but without letting you down."

"And what do you think his involvement is in *the family business?*" Gustav queried sarcastically. "He spent three weeks in the hospital, and almost three month following that, he hardly came in to work at all. If anyone but my son had been so unproductive, they would've been fired long ago. I only keep him on because he is my son, and because I love him, as you rightly said."

"He promised to be your partner when he was only sixteen. He's now a grown thirty-five, and regrets his promise. But he can't break it."

"Oh, is that so? Why didn't he say anything to me about it before?"

"He loved you very much and didn't want to crush your dream."

"My dream?" Gustav laughed. "Did he tell you that? Jesus!"

"You are a businessman, but I am an artist," Maria continued quietly but firmly. "It might sound funny to you, but it sounds normal to me. Nick is very creative. He's a romantic in many ways. He needs to be handled carefully, not like most people. I'm sure he will be a productive writer because it comes from deep in his soul."

"Okay. Finally, now, Mrs. Bell, what are you asking of me?"

"Please, free him from any obligations to you. Tell him and set his mind to follow his heart. Let him go to Europe and write his books. I'll watch over him and can assure you that nothing bad will happen because of his writing. I'll guard against any Gary Edwards getting near him this time. I'll protect your son with tender love and care."

"So, you're really stealing him away from me, is that what you're saying?"

"No, I'm truly returning him to you. You won't lose him. He'll be your loving and beloved son forever. But now he'll be a free and happy son. That's the difference."

"Well…" he thought for a moment. "Well, I would like to hear it from him, in person."

He buzzed his secretary and in a minute Nick entered the office. It was visible that he was a bit confused. Gustav Bell stood up, walked over to his son, placed his hands on Nick's shoulders and looked searchingly into his eyes, startled by the changes he saw.

Nick's eyes shone with such a peaceful light-heartedness and appetite for life. They sparkled with dreams of happiness. Gustav Bell had never in his life seen his son glowing so much with joy and delight before. He almost couldn't recognize this man in front of him. He could clearly see now that Nick was filled with inspiration for the future and was in love. There would be no more suicide attempts for him, for he was saved.

Gustav rested easily in his mind, grateful for this woman who had brought his son back from the abyss. For Nick's sake he was ready to forgive her everything: her age, her foreign accent, her willfulness, her strong mind and womanliness. And most of all, her sabotage of his hope to work along side his son in business. Everything!

He felt satisfied, but first wanted to reprimand his son a little.

"I didn't expect that we would need an envoy between us, Nick. You didn't want to hurt me, but you have by hiding your problem from me all these years. I'm thankful to Maria for her courage to lay her cards on the table and spell it out to me. She is stronger than you, boy."

"Sorry, Dad," Nick's voice quavered.

"Anyway, congratulations!" Gustav Bell gave him a heartfelt hug. "You found exactly the woman you needed. We have to mark that by celebration together. Maria," he said turning to her, "I invite both of you to join me for dinner at the *Astoria*. Right now!"

When Nick and Maria returned to Nick's house late that evening, he said reflectively,

"I just thought... if Gary Edwards hadn't stolen my book, I wouldn't have attempted suicide, and I wouldn't have ever met you. I'm so happy now that I'm even ready to call him to say Thank you."

"I advise against it, Nick. Gary was only one piece of fate in your life," Maria laughed. "Look at my chain of events. If Albert hadn't met the Russian opposition in Moscow twenty-five years ago, I wouldn't have wandered to Minneapolis to meet you, either. I was a married woman, an experienced German journalist at that time and you were a ten-year-old boy in the middle of America. Who could have imagined that our lives could ever have been joined? But fate exists and has its own reasons for helping us find each other. Though, it was something that might have seemed totally impossible."

"I just realized," Nick added, "what my second book will be about."

Chapter 10

IN TWO WEEKS, ALANA RETURNED home from camp where she spent her vacation time with Jessica, Samantha, Bob and some other friends. They were the usual crowd she and Tom had hung out with and she knew them all pretty well. They always had a lot of fun together and being with them usually made Alana happy.

This year, however, her time with them was spoiled because she was pregnant, so she wasn't able to get a very good rest from the city. Every morning Alana felt nauseous and needed to eat something as soon as she got up. Then sometimes she threw up or felt dizzy the whole day. She couldn't stand to drink beer, listen to loud music, play ball, or skateboard. In fact, everything irritated her.

Day in and day out Alana just felt old, sick and miserable. She dreamt of arriving home quickly, having the abortion and getting the whole thing over with - anything to end these disgusting feelings and return to her usual self. She also wanted to end any connection to Nick; she loathed him and his child.

In no time her girlfriends noticed her symptoms. They had had enough life experience to know what it was like to be pregnant. Both of them, Jessica and Samantha, were strongly against Alana getting an abortion.

"Don't you get it, silly girl?" Jessica asked her. "You are in a very lucky position. In fact, this chance only comes once in a lifetime. Not every girl will have such an opportunity. Don't you see? You have hooked a millionaire! Don't even think about an abortion. You'll be set up for life. My God! Can't you just imagine the size of the monthly payment you could get from him? You won't have to work at all. Boy, I sure wish I were in your shoes! Just think, you can buy a beautiful home, enjoy your life, enjoy your baby and find some other man to your liking."

"I'm not sure that that is what I really want," Alana objected. "I truly hate Nick. I don't want to have his baby – or anything else from him. I just want to forget him, quietly marry Tom and to be happy. I want to go on with my police career. Tom and I can have children later."

"No way," Samantha interrupted. "You are really a silly girl. You can have the baby and get money from Nick. Then buy a house and live with Tom. And, on top of it all, you can go on with your career. You will have enough money to hire a nanny who will watch your child. Many rich women do, you know. You'll have lots of choices and lots of freedom. You can have it all! It's as plain as day."

"But I don't want to have or raise a child I don't love. He'll never be happy. He'll know that I hate him. For sure, I'll mess him up good. No, no, forget the whole idea."

"Your child can be sick... or handicapped...or even a full idiot. It doesn't matter; you don't have to be with him. Just get a nanny. It's just perfect, if it happens. I tell you, the money will be outrageous!" Samantha yelled, full of excitement over the possibilities.

"You're against it now because you don't feel well and you hate Nick," Jessica continued. "That's okay. You don't have to like Nick to take his money. He abused you and now he must pay for it. He shouldn't have slept with you without using protection, anyway. It was his mistake an now he must pony up the cash. You just need to find yourself a good lawyer; that's all."

All these discussions were full of mean-spirited advice and Alana was depressed by them. She found them so unbearable that she often ran off into the bushes and cried her heart out, sitting on an old rotten log. It was so hard to listen to this kind of counsel and she already regretted telling her friends the whole truth. It would have been better if she had claimed that she was carrying Tom's baby.

Alana tried to be fair. She knew that Nick couldn't truly be blamed. How could he have prepared condoms when she was the one initiating their encounters? She chose the moments and ambushed him unexpectedly, catching him off-guard and seducing him. The pregnancy was her mistake – she had thought she could win his love through sex. Alana's the one who should have used birth control, but she had been careless and gave no thought to the future. She let her love and excitement to sweep her along, focusing only on the new feelings Nick stirred within her. If she was honest, this entire mess was her fault. But she couldn't admit this to the others.

Alana tried to imagine what her mother would say if she found out about these discussions with the girls. Sure as hell, Maria would tell her that to get money from a man this way was both dishonest and mean. And it didn't matter how rich the man was.

At the same time, Alana knew that her mother dreamt about grand-children. She would never accept the idea of an abortion and would offer to help raise the child. That was exactly what Alana didn't want to have happen. The more she thought about the matter, the more she determined to not to tell her mother anything and quietly have the abortion.

Besides her own troubles interfering with a pleasant vacation at camp, the long-time relationship between Samantha and Jessica was dramatically ruptured.

Alana wasn't personally involved in their falling out but she witnessed the whole dreadful thing. Her nerves and soul were shaken and her misery increased.

One day at camp, Jessica caught her boyfriend, Bob, who had returned from Afghanistan two months earlier, in bed with her best friend Samantha. Jessica was shocked and outraged and ran away from the camp to the bushes, where she found Alana sitting alone on a log and crying. The girls hugged and cried together, charging life with injustice, men with cruelty, and friends with infidelity. United in crisis, they decided to revenge themselves on the men of the world – starting with Nick. They would keep Alana's baby, go to court and get Nick's money, rent an apartment together and raise the child.

With this spontaneous decision, Alana and Jessica left camp together. Alana drove her friend home. On the way, they looked at some small walk-up apartments and located one to rent quite easily. They decided to move as soon as possible. Alana was ready to do it in the next few days, in order to hide her pregnancy from her mother. Jessica also was impatient to re-locate from the place she had been sharing with Bob.

When Alana reached her *River Valley* suite, she was surprised that her mother wasn't home. The place looked dead and empty, as if something was missing.

Alana took off her backpack, and then walked around the rooms, trying to understand why everything felt so desolate. She caught it easily: the living room walls were bare and all of Maria's paintings were gone.

Where could they be? Alana thought. Had she finally gotten tired of them? It's probably because Uncle Albert had died. She had always painted for and about him.

The truth was that Alana had never liked her mother's art. She couldn't understand it and had little interest in trying to. Most of the images scared her. They gave her shivers when she looked at them. She was always ashamed to let her friends see them.

On the night Nick had come to the place, she hadn't turned on the living room lights for that very reason. The last thing she wanted was for him to see them. She had always sensed that something bad could happen because of the paintings. In some senses, she was even jealous of them.

Well, now they were gone and Alana was glad. It helped her relax and calm down.

She surveyed the rooms more attentively and found that many things were gone or packed in boxes, as if for moving. It looked like Maria had the same idea as she did.

Maybe mom is getting ready to move with her boyfriend, Alana thought. That would be good for me, because then she would have no objections to my moving out. She would be pre-occupied with her old guy and his arthritis. That's cute. I'm happy for her.

Then Alana went out into the lobby to check the mail. The box was full of junk mail and fliers. Alana realized that her mother hadn't emptied it for some time. She probably had been absent some days, as well. Suddenly, stuck between two envelopes, Alana saw a letter addressed to her. It was from the police officer responsible for her case.

The letter notified Miss Alana Miller that Mr. Gary Edwards had generously refused to press any charges against her for her uncivil behavior on *The Georgia Show*.

This girl is still a child who has probably fallen under the influence of one of my enemies, his statement read. *I am sure she already regrets her hasty and unjustified action and will never do it again. When she understands that I forgive her, she will see what the real generosity of a genius is.*

The quote in the letter was from one of Gary's TV interviews.

Alana felt ashamed of her impulsive, childish public act.

Maybe Gary is not so bad, she thought. I don't know who to believe anymore. Nick once looked so open and sincere, but he was quite rude to me after all the help I gave him. He is the ungrateful pig in this story! Gary looked like the mean thief, but now he's so kind to me.

I'm so sorry I ever got involved in their sick relationship. What I did for Nick, I now regret. I feel that I need to apologize to Gary and thank him for his kindness. I'm also ready to spite Nick and make him go through the same pain as I did with him. He will have to pay!

Alana looked in the phone book and found the number of the TV station. When she called, the receptionist gave her the number of *The Georgia Show* producer. A few minutes later she was on the line with the show assistant, Judy Rolls.

"My name is Alana Miller," she said. "I'm the girl who spit in Gary Edwards' face on your show a few months back. You probably remember me. I'm also the girlfriend of Nick Bell. I know the connection between his unpublished book and Gary Edwards' *My Obsessive Passion*.

About three month ago, you called Nick Bell and invited both of us to be guests on your show. At that time we weren't interested, but now I've changed my mind. I would be happy to tell your audience the story of my relationship with Nick Bell and his book. I want to explain why I spat in Gary Edwards' face, and apologize to him, as well."

"This is amazing!" exclaimed Judy. "You are a real godsend! You can't imagine how much Georgia is interested in you. We were trying to locate you for a long time. What are your plans for tomorrow? I will send a film crew to your home."

"Not tomorrow, please," Alana said. "I just returned from vacation. I'm not quite ready yet. Maybe in a few days. Okay?"

Alana already knew that she was working night shifts the coming week. So, she arranged an appointment with the film crew at 8 A.M. in three days' time. She would just be arriving home from work then and it would be the most comfortable situation for her.

I'm glad that I'm still living in this beautiful building, she thought. When I move to my walk-up, it wouldn't look very good on TV.

Excited with dreams of fame and revenge, Alana took a shower and stretched out on her bed to relax. Today, she finally felt a bit better. That gave her hope. The doctor had already informed her that after some weeks, her pregnancy wouldn't be so hard to bear. It seemed to be true.

Alana was lying on her bed and thinking about Nick. Of course, she still loved him but it now twisted into hate following his rejection of her. Her fragile feelings were offended and hurt, but still deep down she wanted him and was sure she would love him forever. If he came back to her, or even called her, she would gladly forgive everything and run to his arms in a split second.

Alana had no idea if it could ever happen, but she didn't want to give up hoping and dreaming about it.

Samantha had told me that, in her opinion, Nick is seeing someone else, Alana thought. I don't know if Samantha is right or not, because she is such a bitch and often judging people based on her own behavior. But it is possible that he has another woman, of course. His secretary is so young, with a charming voice. Also, those professional women who were with him that night were pretty and in his circle. Sure, he has lots of choices besides me. How can I possess and protect him from them all? Every woman who sees him will want him because he is so amazing.

In many ways, it's so difficult to have a lover like him. It's impossible to put him in a cage. Jessica's right – the only way to catch him is to trap him with the baby. I'll have to play this card and then he'll be mine.

Alana believed that her appearance on *The Georgia Show*, where she would publicly announce that she was carrying Nick's child, would be helpful in this direction. These thoughts gave her more confidence and a sense of victory.

While Alana was resting, she heard the door unlock and her mother appeared in the corridor.

"Mom!" she shouted, jumping up from her bed and running to her.

Maria was standing beside the door, dressed in a long black skirt and blue top, clutching a huge bouquet of white lilies. She looked tired, with big black circles under her eyes, but her face radiated happiness at the same time. Her eyes shone with a special inner light and her lips broke into a little smile at the corners. It was her, and it wasn't her at the same time.

Alana wanted to give Maria a big hug, but stopped immediately, not recognizing her.

"Mom!" she exclaimed. "You look strange. You look ten years younger than usual, but so exhausted, like you had a week of non-stop sex or something. Is your new boyfriend really such a stud?"

"Yes," Maria whispered, confused. "I can't hug you, sweetie. Let me put these flowers on the table."

"They smell fantastic! Are they another present from him?"

Maria just nodded. She went to the kitchen, filled a clay jar with water and put the lilies in.

"Has he proposed to you yet?" Alana asked, following her to the kitchen.

"Yes, sweetie," Maria turned, put her arms around her daughter and started crying.

"Mo-om! Stop crying, please," Alana begged her and fondly patted her back. "You shouldn't be so sensitive. What's the problem? I know everything. I noticed you had been packing some stuff already. I realize you want to move in with him. It's okay with me. He is probably rich and then you won't need to work so hard. It's all for the best.

"I know, Mom, that you're scared to hurt me by spelling it out. I understand that I have to leave this suite, too, because it's connected to your work here. It's all right, don't worry about me. I just wanted to tell you that I've already decided to move in with Jessica. So, you see, we've got perfect timing on this thing."

"Really?" Maria looked at her guiltily.

"Yes, Mom. Promise that you won't worry about me. I'm happy that you have your own life at last. It'll work out great for both of us. It's the best way, Mom. Don't you see? And please stop crying. Let's talk about your future. Did he give you a ring?"

Maria put out her hand and showed Alana her ring.

"Wow! Five diamonds? Is he really so rich? I heard from some people that he's a little stingy, but I already told you about that. It is strange how some people spread rumors about others. It looks like he's really a generous guy! Or is it only because he's so much in love? What's the truth, Mom?"

"A little of both," Maria admitted, lowering her glance. She couldn't bear to look directly into Alana's eyes.

"Of course, you are young compared to him," Alana laughed. "It's a really good thing for you, Mom, that you met this old one. When do you plan to move out?"

"This Saturday. We are going on our honeymoon in Europe. We'll have our wedding somewhere over there, when we find a beautiful church. Then, when we return, I'll live at his place. So, I quit my job and I am supposed to leave this apartment, of course."

"A wedding in Europe! My gosh, Mom! I want to come, too. You wouldn't get married without me, would you? Ask him, please, to buy me a ticket, too. Please, Mo-om!"

"I...I'll try. I'll ask him..." Maria stammered. "I promise...I'll ask him, sweetie."

She really couldn't imagine how to get out of this tight corner.

"Let's...let's cook some dinner, sweetie. I won't be going anywhere these next three days. It'll be time for us to be together. I'll be with you, I promise. I was staying at his place, but I came home especially to see you. Now, tell me your story. How was camping? Did you have a good time with your friends? How are they doing?

"By the way, Tom did call twice. I talked to him briefly. He's okay and has only two months of service left so he'll be back at the end of October. He's really looking forward to seeing you again. I told him, as you requested, that you love him. He also asked me to pass on a kiss from him."

Maria kissed Alana's cheek and smiled. The tension of the moment had almost passed. They scoured the refrigerator and cupboards and threw some things together to make a dinner. While cooking and eating side by side, they chatted as usual – like best friends. It seemed as though nothing had changed in their lives.

Alana told her mother about the Jessica-Bob-Samantha love triangle which had really upset her.

"You know, Mom, it stressed me almost as much as it did Jessica," she said worriedly. "I've known them all since high school. Jess and Sam were best friends since first grade. How could Samantha even think of setting her eyes on a boy who was already taken? Couldn't she find one who was free? She's really a bitch to steal her best friend's guy! Jess trusted her. It's so horribly mean what she did to her. Don't you agree, Mom?"

Maria listened to her daughter in silence.

"I don't know, sweetie," she finally offered. "It's not good to blame people. You don't really know the whole story. Maybe Bob isn't in love with Jessica at all. Maybe Samantha is his true love. Nobody but they could know that. Neither of them is really bad or good. They are just people living Life."

"It's strange, Mom," Alana ventured. "You were always so old-fashioned before, so moral. Things like that used to always irritate you. Now, with your own lover, you sound very different. Did he have a girlfriend before you, and then you seduced him away from her? I really doubt it, because he's so old and not at all good-looking. Sorry to say that. But I'm still curious."

Maria bit her lips. She turned pale and glanced away, not daring to catch Alana's eye.

"About my man..." she said quietly, "...yes, he had a woman before me. He actually had many women, as far as I know."

"Of course," Alana insisted. "He's had a long life! I'm not talking about all his women in the past. I mean now. Did you happen to steal him away from somebody, too?"

Maria's face quivered. "I think so," she said, taking a deep breath. "But I can't judge him – or myself. He just fell in love with me, and I did the same with him."

"No wonder," Alana lightened up. "You are still pretty. But his other girlfriend was probably an old witch."

"Alana, you are too light-headed, I fear. You find pinning labels and judging people far too easy," Maria's voice was shaky. "Sometimes feelings get out of control and are not so effortless to understand. And some things in life are fated and almost impossible to resist. Of course, I'm sorry about his previous woman, but it can't be helped. What happened - happened. Nobody is bad or guilty."

"Don't worry, Mom," Alana said. "I'm not blaming you. Relax. Don't be so nervous. Look at you! You're ready to faint. Why? Just forget about his unlucky old witch. You're going to be *a bride!* Have you decided on a dress? Do you want a white or a colored one?"

"I dream of a light blue one," Maria said, taking a deep breath again. "You know, that color is holy for me. It was the first color I saw when I opened my eyes and returned to life at St. Peter's Cathedral in Berlin. The sunshine was streaming in through the stained glass blue windows."

"It's so romantic! I really want to be with you at your wedding!" Alana exclaimed happily. "You can't have a wedding without your only daughter being there. Did Stan have kids? Will they attend your wedding?"

"No, he didn't."

"How come? Was he married before?"

"Yes."

"Many years ago? Is his wife dead?"

"No, they are divorced."

"Because he can't have kids, I'll bet. It's understandable. Lucky you, Mom. Nobody else will get his inheritance then."

"Stop it, please, sweetie," Maria begged her, her voice filled with unhappiness. "That sounds awful. I care absolutely nothing for his money."

"I know, Mom. I was just teasing you. I didn't ever care about Nick's money, either. I just loved him because he was so amazing. But now the situation has changed. You know, I stopped dating him. We fought and he was so mean to me!"

"Really?" Maria was pained to hear this. "What did he say or do that was so mean?"

"He asked me to leave him alone and to stop chasing him."

"Well, what's so mean about that?"

"It's totally unfair! I loved and wanted him. I was dying from love for him."

"Why was it his fault if he doesn't love you? It's nobody's fault. It's beyond your control. He couldn't force himself to love you. You are a big girl already and should understand how a man behaves toward you. If you want to be successful with the guys, you shouldn't be the initiator. If a man is attracted or loves you, he'll set the wheels in motion. It's natural. That's how biology set it up. And, if he doesn't take the initiative, it simply means he doesn't love you. So, you'd better not even waste your time on him. Please, believe me. I'm telling you this from my open heart and life experience.

"That's why I always thought Tom was the best man for you," Maria continued. "I can see that he is devoted to you. That's all that is important to me. Instead, you chased a beautiful vision and failed to appreciate Tom's love. Now, it's probably time to correct your compass. I pray that Tom returns safely, you two get married and live happily ever after."

Alana heard her mother's advice but couldn't unburden her own soul to her. It was a good time to let Maria know about her ill-timed pregnancy, but she had no courage to speak. She decided she would only reveal the truth on *The Georgia Show*. Her mind was made up. She would prove Nick's paternity with a test and get his millions for her child – the route her friends had convinced her to take.

"I think it's you who has the beautiful illusions about life, Mom," Alana finally spoke. "You are too naïve! Life is not as sweet and kind as you think. Jessica and Samantha's spat hurt me a lot. I understand now that it's impossible to trust anyone, even if you're good friends! Even someone you've known a long time can't be trusted not to stab you in the back. Look at Nick's case with Gary Edwards. But Sam's betrayal of Jessica was much closer to me – and all the more real and shocking!"

Alana sat down beside her mother and gave her a big, heartfelt hug.

"There's no one left for me to trust – or love in this world – except you, Mom," she said sadly, placing her head on Maria's shoulder. "You are the only person who is honorable in my eyes – the only person who cares for me more than herself. I trust you completely, Mom. That's what real love is. I know you will never let me down."

"Thank you, Alana," Maria whispered tearfully, "but I'm afraid you overrate me. I'm not as perfect as you suppose."

"Come on, Mom. Your little sexual tricks with your old boyfriend don't lower you at all in my sight. You've survived a lot and you suffered for many years. That certainly counts for something."

"You can't imagine, sweetie, how I'm suffering now," Maria added, and pulled her daughter closer to her. "I feel like I'm on a torture rack for all the heartache you're enduring."

"Why? Is it because we won't be living together anymore? It's not a problem, Mom, believe me. All the girls I know have been on their own for several years now. I'm the only one who's still 'at home', so to speak. After all, I'm twenty-two. I stuck with you so long because we were both so poor and I really couldn't afford my own rent. Now I've found a way to solve this problem, to get money for my education and many nice things, besides. I'll be okay. And I want you to be happy, too, with your new husband. Promise never to worry about me again. Okay, Mom?"

"I'll try, sweetie. But please promise me to be more level-headed and serious. Don't do anything crazy again, like that stunt you pulled on that damn TV show."

"Okay, okay," Alana convinced her, while a mischievous smile flitted cross her face. "I'm absolutely level-headed now, believe me, Mom."

For the next two days, the two women packed and reorganized their lives, dividing up their common household. Most of their stuff, like the furniture, TV, dishes, pots and pans, and houseplants went to Alana to start her new independent life. It would increase her moving expenses but help her set up house more easily. Maria packed just two good-sized

136

boxes for herself of the things which were especially dear to her. Of course, she also took her painting supplies.

Maria had already discussed her move with Nick. They had decided that his caretaker Bob would drive him over to *River Valley* the night before their honeymoon departure, then return to Nick's house with her boxes.

As Alana organized her relocation, she prepared the bulk of her belongings for the moving van. But she sometimes left the apartment with some fragile items she wanted to drive to her new place herself. Maria used these infrequent breaks to furtively phone Nick.

"Little dolly! Finally!" he breathed with relief. "Do you know what I'm doing now? I'm looking at your paintings. I found some more ideas I can use in my book. I'll show you later."

"Okay, my love," Maria responded. "I miss you so much."

"Me, too. You can't imagine how much! I'm counting the hours – no, minutes – until I can hug you again. I can't wait!"

"How's your writing coming along?" Maria inquired.

"Really well. It's the only thing that fills my life when you're not beside me. I've finish putting the plot together now. I've also written some parts that will go to the middle. But I'm still frantically searching for a good title for the book. And I need some fresh ideas for a perfect ending. I want something strong and impressive to end with. Would you like to hear some of it?"

"Yes, my love. I really want…"

Last week, when Maria stayed at Nick's house, he had started his second book.

They had discussed the story, ideas, dramatic lines, characters and climatic points whenever they took breaks from lovemaking and were relaxing on the bed together. They also talked about the book when they took pleasant hand-in-hand walks in the fragrant pine forest behind Nick's house. It was again the topic of discussion at their meals at home or lunches and dinners in restaurants. Some of their deepest ideas for it emerged as they gazed, mesmerized, at Maria's paintings which now hung throughout Nick's spacious home. Already 'the book' was like a familiar member of the family, their mutual 'child'. It was their dearest baby who was a product of their united souls.

After this intense prelude, Nick began to put words on paper.

Sometimes, he would sit in his armchair and write on his laptop, positioned on the coffee table in front of him. Maria would curl up on the floor beside him, resting her head on his lap and drinking in his specialty. She was awed by his inspiration and passion for work. He radiated talent and spirituality and she found it hard to tear her eyes away from him. Maria couldn't believe she actually deserved to be so deliriously happy with him and was truly spellbound by these moments sent from above.

Maria had asked Nick to let her spend her last few days prior leaving with Alana. Before she returned to her suite, he pulled her into his garden and cut all the white lilies growing there.

"That should be enough for you, little dolly, to smell for three days and think of me," he declared ardently. "I'll continue writing, don't worry. But you have to call me whenever you can. I can't call you, you know that."

"Yes," Maria murmured, as she clung to him. "Sorry, my love. I'm really sorry."

They both avoided talking about Alana because the topic was too painful for them. In truth, neither of them knew how to handle it. They tried their best not to mention her name and not to think about her, to sidestep the guilt that threatened to overwhelm them both.

It would just be better to reveal the truth to my poor girl, Maria pondered, sometimes. I'm bending over backwards not to lie to her. I haven't lied once. Alana doesn't really suspect a thing, but I just can imagine her total shock if she find out. Oh God, please help me! Forgive me, but I can't bring myself to break the news to her.

Maria convinced herself that she was sparing Alana's feelings by keeping her secret from her. For now, it looked as though separation would be the best solution.

Then time would serve as the best doctor, to heal her wounded soul, Maria despairingly thought. What else can I do? Alana will live on her own; she won't see Nick anymore and will be able to forget him. Step-by-step, everything will turn out okay. Then Tom will come back and fill up her life again. He truly loves her and will be able to cure her lovesickness. I'm sure everything will be all right.

If Alana and Tom marry soon, Maria planned to send them honeymoon tickets as a wedding present. Then the younger couple could join them in Europe and everyone would be reconciled. She dreamt to reunite her family and see her future grandchildren one day. But for now, she must remain silent. It was the only option she felt she had. There was no other way to cut the knot.

So Maria was only able to phone Nick when her daughter was out. They had charming, flirtatious conversations. She listened with great interest as he shared some fragments from his latest writing. Maria was happy talking with him, but at the same time felt tense and scared that Alana would return at any minute and burst in on their covert communications. She felt terrible, as though she were a thief or some sort. Maria hated living with guilty conscience and started counting the minutes before she and Nick would fly away to their new future.

The evening before their departure finally arrived. Alana brought home a bottle of champagne to celebrate her mother's marriage and the end of their years together.

"Let's drink a farewell toast, Mom," she said dolefully, pouring some bubbly into glasses. "I can't drink a lot because I'm leaving for work soon. But you can have as much as you want. Where's your old man anyway? Why doesn't he come by to say bye to me?"

"Sorry, he's busy this evening. I can say bye to him from you," Maria replied. "We are leaving at five in the morning. Our plane departs at seven. Then, we'll change planes in New York. When I find out the day of our wedding, I'll call you. I'll really try to send you a ticket. And you, sweetie, please behave. Be grown up and confident. You'd better wait for Tom and be happy with him. Give him a hug from his 'mom' for me, will you?"

"I will," Alana nodded. "I wish you every happiness Mom. You really deserve it. I love you, Mom and I'll miss you." She kissed Maria affectionately on the cheek. "Call me from some of your hotels. That's the only way we can stay in touch. I gave you my new number, didn't I?"

"Yes, I've got it. I'll call you, sweetie, I promise. You are my child, my only flesh and blood."

"Well, you'll have a new husband and family soon," Alana teased her.

"That's very different, dear," Maria drank her champagne but was chocked with emotion over the moment. They sat looking at each other with love, pity and regret: things would never be the same again.

At eleven o'clock Alana changed into her uniform and got ready for work.

"I'll come by tomorrow morning after work and pick up the small stuff," she said to Maria. "At noon the moving van will come. Then, I'll return the building keys, the garage opener and your cell phone to *West-Build Management*. Don't worry, Mom. I'll take care of everything. Enjoy your honeymoon and your new life."

"Thanks, sweetie," Maria said, seeing her off. "I'm going to get some sleep now. I'm really tired and I need to get up early to catch my flight."

"Will your old man drive you to airport?"

"No. We won't be able to leave the car there for an indefinite period of time. So we'll just take a taxi."

"Good idea. Bye, Mom!" Alana waved as she stepped on to the elevator down to the parking garage.

As she neared her car, she saw a dusty while sedan pull in and an old, crooked, lame man getting out with some difficulty. He was nice, with a kind, wrinkled face and a bushy gray moustache. Alana had seen him before and always stopped to chat with him. It was the nearly deaf Stan from the twelfth floor who – as far as she could tell – was going to be her stepfather now.

Oh, good thing I ran in to him, she thought. Now I can congratulate him properly.

Stan opened the trunk of his car and was starting to take out some bags and suitcases. It was difficult because they were heavy and he moved so slowly.

"Hi, Stan," Alana greeted him cheerfully. "How are you this evening?"

"I'm fine. Thank you. What about you, Miss Alana?" he answered her in his rasping voice.

"I'm okay. Do you need any help?"

"No. Thank you. I'm not in any hurry. You're on your way out, I see."

"Yes, I'm going to work now."

"So, I don't want to make you late."

"I guess I won't have another chance to see you before you leave," Alana said. "So I want to give you my congratulations and wish you every blessing. I hope you'll have an amazing time and will be very happy."

She gave him a sincere hug.

"Thank you, Miss Alana. Thank you, my dear," Stan said, a bit bewildered. He was looking inside his trunk for something. Then he pulled out a plastic bag of fresh-picked oranges.

"These are for you, Miss Alana," he said. "I picked these especially for your mom. But you can take them for a snack at work."

"Thank you very much, Stan," she smiled as she took the bag. "They'll be great, I'm sure. You are so generous, as I know. Thank you for everything you've done for us."

"You are very welcome," said a beaming Stan.

He ran his fingers over his hood, looked at them, and shook his head with dismay.

"My car is so damn dusty," he noted. "Well it's late now, so I'll wash it tomorrow morning. Bye Miss Alana. Don't work too hard!"

Alana put the bag of oranges in her back seat and waved to Stan as she pulled out of her stall.

He's really a charming gent, she thought light-heartedly. They'll make a nice couple!

Chapter 11

W<small>HILE</small> A<small>LANA</small> <small>WAS ON VACATION</small>, many things changed at St. Boniface. The hospital got ready to host an international scientific conference on cancer research, which was scheduled for this weekend in the conference hall located on the top floor.

Volunteers had decorated the walls of the main entrance with balloons and flower garlands and they added more artificial trees in the lobby. In the center of the lobby was Fall Charitable Art Exhibition featuring works from clay, metal, glass, plastic, fabric, dry flowers and leaves. The money raised from the sale of this art would go for further cancer research. All in all, the hospital had taken on the festive air of a grand occasion.

The additional activity in the lobby during the day created extra work for the security guards, but at 11 P.M. all of the doors were automatically locked and alarms were set. Visitors and outpatient staff were long gone. Even the receptionist from the main desk in the lobby left at midnight. Only the night nurses, resident doctors, paramedics awaiting emergency calls and the security staff remained to keep watch over the patients, most them sound asleep.

It was very quiet. Nobody approached the exhibition and nobody needed to be guarded. Alana wandered alone around the lobby and looked things over curiously.

It was the first time, since she began working at the hospital, that Alana felt absolutely lonely, tired and unhappy. She attributed this partly to her physical condition and now realized she should not have agreed to do night shifts during her pregnancy. Another mistake she had made was to drink some champagne with her mother, against her doctor's advice. She had been so saddened to see her mother leave that she had momentarily forgotten herself. Now she was feeling dizzy and nauseous because of that half a glass of champagne.

Alana even felt that she would be unable to do her regular patrol work around the building tonight. She sank into a visitor armchair in the foyer, beside the reception desk, closed her eyes and thought about her mother.

As a child, Alana hadn't been with Maria very much. Uncle Albert and Aunt Luisa basically raised her. She lived at their home and at their store, which were located in the same building. Maria lived there as well, but she was away at work all the time – left early while Alana was still sleeping and returned home late after her daughter had gone to bed again. Sometimes, in the darkness, Alana felt a motherly peck on her cheek or a kindly pat on the head as a goodbye or hello. She knew by the smell and warmth that it was her mother, coming and going.

"Bye, Mom. Love you," she mumbled in her sleep, turned over and pulled her covers up. It was enough socializing for them both. They each knew the other existed and is full of love.

Any additional messages between them were relayed through Albert and Luisa.

"Your mom will be home late, sweetie," Luisa often told her. "She got an extra job cleaning suites at an apartment building."

"Okay, Auntie Luisa. Just read me a story before I go to sleep, please."

Or Albert would say, "Little dolly, did you know that Alana's school grades aren't very good this year? Yesterday we went to a conference at her school and talked to her teacher."

"Really? Albert, can you please help her? Check her homework, especially in math. You know what to do. You're educated enough. Please..."

Albert and Luisa were Alana's real parents up to the age of twelve. Then, Maria finally found a resident manager position and was able to live in the building where she worked. Alana relocated with her, and it was just in time. By now Luisa was so handicapped that she was wheelchair bound. Albert had a lot on his shoulders, taking care of his wife and looking after their German food business. In addition, he did the heavier work at Maria's new building. None of this was easy for him since he was already past sixty and didn't feel younger than his age, like Maria did.

Over the last ten years, Maria worked at three different buildings. As her experience grew she moved up the ladder. She began in a small walk-up, and then moved to a six storey apartment building and finally, to a first-class condominium high-rise, *River Valley*.

Alana lived with her during that time. They were best friends; the foundation of their relationship was one of freedom. Even living together, mother and daughter each had their own personal life. Neither dominated the other, and they went out of their way not to interfere with each other's business and privacy.

Sometimes, Alana went camping with her friends or visited Tom's family in Duluth, but all those trips were brief – two weeks, at the most. In truth, this would now be the first real parting between the two women. The idea of the whole year separation, especially with a child on the way and a lawsuit looming, would be a severe test of Alana's maturity and true independence. The plan scared her, while also filling her with pride that she would have a chance to prove herself. Again, she was thankful she hadn't shared her secret with Maria. Alana believed she'll be able to confidently manage her own future.

If only she felt better! With this dizziness and weakness it would be impossible to work nights. Alana decided she'd better call her supervisor tomorrow and have her schedule changed.

Around 3 A.M. Alana began feeling especially nauseous and realized it would be a good time to have something to eat. She took the elevator to the underground parking area and grabbed the sack of oranges from her car. Then she went into the security office where Jim, Ramesh and a new girl, Nancy, were sitting.

Nancy was hired only a week ago, during Alana's vacation. She was a twenty-year-old mulatto with many tiny braids. She was sexy and pretty and Jim and Ramesh were quite taken with her.

The three of them were having a snack break. Coffee was brewing and the aroma filled the small room. On the table were turkey sandwiches, which Jim usually brought from his grandma's farm and spicy Indian pies, which Ramesh's mother always baked for his snack at work.

"Join us," Jim invited Alana as she entered. "We're having potluck because Nancy forgot her lunch. Ohhhh! Your bag looks weighty. What've you got there?"

"Oranges," Alana said as she opened the bag on the table.

"Why did you bring so many?" Ramesh asked.

"Oh, it was just accidental. They were a gift from my stepfather-to-be."

Jim selected one orange and looked at it attentively.

"It looks strange," he observed. "It's kind of dusty. There's some kind of pollen on it."

"That's because they're from the tree – not the store," Alana explained. "He picks them usually on his way home from Arizona when he visits his kids."

"I can wash them," Nancy suggested.

"I'll help you!" Jim exclaimed readily.

"I have a knife. We can cut up some," Ramesh proposed and ran to catch them.

The three of them started on the oranges, but Alana stood on the sidelines. She sat down in the nearest chair, her mind working a mile a minute. What was it she'd just said? What did it mean?

She now recalled that every year Stan had returned from Arizona with oranges for them. He always told them that he'd been in the Southwest visiting his kids. Yes, that was the story he repeated quite often.

But then, Alana thought, mom had said that her new husband had no children – and so they wouldn't attend the European wedding. But Stan *does* have kids! There is some kind of misunderstanding somewhere. Did I hear my mother right? Or maybe, Stan's kids are adopted and mom didn't consider them part of the family? It is all so confusing.

Alana's mind desperately searched for any kind of halfway reasonable explanation, even this one she knew was plainly silly. She knitted her brows, trying to focus on details of her encounter with Stan this evening. His car was very dusty and looked like he had returned from a long drive somewhere. "I'll wash it tomorrow morning," he'd said.

But, how could he wash the car in the morning if he was leaving with mom at 5 A.M. for the airport? Alana reckoned. Nobody wakes up at four in the morning to wash a car, do they? It was only possible for a young and healthy man to do such a thing, but Stan is old and tired. I just don't get it.

Stan's car was dusty. He had a lot of luggage. He brought oranges. All of this pointed to the fact that he had just returned from his annual extended trip to see his kids in Arizona, Alana kept thinking. That means he wouldn't have been around for the past two months. But, then, who gave mom the flowers, presents – and the ring? Maybe Stan was a skinflint after all. Certainly, someone else had been courting mom.

Now that she thought about it, it was surely some other man in her mother's life. Alana remembered her mother's sparkling eyes, her estranged look, the black circles of exhaustion under her eyes and how Maria radiated such happiness and satisfaction. Alana had teased her mother about a week of sex, but she now realized that it was the truth. Her lover couldn't be Stan, who was near eighty. There had to be a younger man in the picture somewhere, maybe Maria's age or even younger - someone who was virile and turned on by her mother.

Alana laughed. She knew there were a lot of single men in the building. It was funny. How could she have been so wide of the mark in thinking it was Stan? How could she have been so foolish? She had always teased her mother about Stan, and Maria had played along with the game.

But why didn't mom ever protest – or correct me? Alana's next thought was. Why couldn't she simply have said, 'You, silly girl! It's not

Stan at all, but John from the fifth floor or Mike from the eleventh?' She just kept her secret and let me think it was Stan. I wonder why?

It was all so weird and confusing.

Maybe mom was just teasing me in return, Alana guessed. Maybe she was joking. But it's a strange thing to joke about and mom didn't act like she was kidding me. She always looked a bit confused when I pressed her for information or asked too direct questions about her man. She even cried sometimes. What was going on here? Why was she so uncomfortable talking about him? What was she trying to hide?

There must be some kind of mystery connected with this man, something extraordinary about him. Could he be handicapped? Or maybe he's black – or yellow? Maybe he was just released from prison? Maybe he's homeless or a poor immigrant, too? Not likely! Look at the presents and flowers! And flying to Europe for a honeymoon. The man was supposed to be – in fact, must be rich.

Then again, maybe it was… a woman? Maybe mom hooked up with a lesbian and that made it very hard for her to tell me about it? Obviously she avoided telling me the truth, or even giving me many clues to go on. Why? She knows me – I'm not judgmental. I understand everything and mom knows that.

"Alana, wake up and have an orange," she suddenly heard Nancy's voice. It brought her musings back to reality. Nancy stood in front of her and thrust a paper plate with orange sections on it toward her. "Take some," she said, smiling. "They are very juicy and fresh. No comparison with supermarket fruit. Thank your stepfather for us."

"I will," Alana said feebly, taking a slice and sucking on it. It really was juicy and sweet. It succored her suppress her nausea. She enjoyed it and helped herself to some more, but her mind was not with her colleagues.

"You're some kind of zombie tonight, Alana," Jim noticed. "What happened? Family problems or just a headache?"

"Yeah…" Alana answered uncertainly. "I need to call my mom."

"Come on," teased Jim. "You've got to be kidding! It's a quarter to four in the morning. She'll be asleep. Don't disturb her."

"No, I'm serious. It's an emergency. She's supposed to wake up at four anyway, because she's leaving for the airport at dawn."

Alana dialed the number, but reached only the answering machine. She dialed three more times, all with the same results, and finally decided to leave a message.

"Mom," she said. "It's me. Please call me back at St. Boniface's right away. It's really important. Just call me as soon as you wake up. I need to talk to you. I have to understand something important. Please, Mom."

Alana hung up and sat silently beside the phone. Her mind wouldn't stop its whirling dance. What was going on? What was her mother concealing from her? During their whole life together, they had been understanding and supportive friends. There had never been any reason to hide anything from each other. There must be some really horrible reason, something terrible coming between them!

Alana couldn't hold her emotions back. She tensely awaited Maria's phone call but the phone was silent.

The guys beside her were eating, drinking coffee, joking and laughing but Alana was in her own space. She couldn't concentrate on reality. Instead, her mind was filled with far-fetched possibilities.

The phone rang at two minutes to four and she jumped up like a crazy woman and grabbed the receiver.

"Hi, guys. Could you sign me out, please?" It was Tracy who was on patient watch on the third floor. "I'm leaving now."

A lightening bolt struck Alana.

"Tracy!" she shouted into the phone. "Can you possibly relieve me until eight? I really have to go home. It's urgent. I'll pay you cash."

"Mmmm..." Tracy thought for a minute. "Okay. Ten dollars an hour," she said.

"Okay. I'll leave the money with Jim. Thanks."

With unsteady hands, Alana pulled out her wallet, took four ten dollar bills and handed them to Jim. Her workmates stood in silence, watching her. It began to dawn on them that something serious was afoot. She wanted to tell them good bye, but couldn't find the words for her trembling lips.

"Don't worry. Just go," Jim urged. "I'll call and report the change to the center. Good luck!"

Alana ran for the elevator and raced to her car. St. Boniface wasn't far from her home, only a fifteen minute drive. She sped through the early morning streets, gripping the steering wheel with both her shaky hands. At a quarter after four she pulled into the *River Valley* garage and dashed to the apartment.

Alana paused at the door before entering the suite, taking a deep breath and trying to reduce the panic seizing her. Then, very deliberately, she put her key in the lock and quietly opened the door. Then she remained standing in silence in the entryway. Things were dark, but the hallway light cast some illumination through the open door and fell on two leather suitcases and a travel bag waiting there.

At first Alana surmised that Maria had overslept and had missed the alarm. Then she noticed a pair of man's sandals by the suitcases and understood that her mother was not alone. Alana's eyes went down the left corridor and saw that Maria's bedroom door was slightly ajar, and a nightlight was on in the room. She tiptoed closer and could hear the hushed voice of her mother speaking to someone. Sure as hell, the newlyweds were in bed together.

Shaky with impatience and dread, Alana lurked outside the bedroom door awhile and then, confident they didn't know she was there, ventured a peek inside. She saw a naked man, his shoulders and back torso. His face was buried in Maria's breasts, kissing them lovingly. Alana saw her mother's hands caressing the man's head and blocking any view of his hair. Her mother's eyes were closed, and there was such a fantastic heavenly expression on her face. The pair was obviously relaxing in the afterglow of their pleasure.

It's not a woman! It's a man...not black...and not handicapped, Alana thought.

One by one her imagined scenarios crumbled, as she spied breathlessly into the murky darkness. Who was he, after all? Then Maria opened her eyes and glanced at the clock.

"It's already past four, my love," she whispered tenderly. "We haven't slept all night. Now we need to go. I guess we can get some sleep during our flight."

"Just a bit more, little dolly," the man answered. "I missed you so badly these past three days. If you hadn't called me so often, I don't think I could have survived. And now, when I know that I won't be able to freely caress you for twelve hours on the plane..."

Alana stood stone still. She realized that she knew this man's voice very well. It was very familiar to her, in fact. Familiar with pain!

But before the voice could even register, his words hit her smack in the face.

Little dolly?! she thought, still not understanding who was in front of her eyes. How come? Only Uncle Albert called mom that name...

"You shouldn't be so greedy, Nick," Maria teased him playfully. "Leave something for yourself for later."

At these words, Alana grabbed the door frame, fearful of fainting. Her brain was pierced by lightening bolts. Nick?! How many men in the world are named Nick? It was *his* voice. It was *him!!!*

Nick and...mom! Mom and...Nick! No, it's unthinkable! It's totally impossible! No, I love him...I'm pregnant with his child...Mo-om!!! Alana's brain exploded, shattering any rational thought and unleashing ricocheting emotional extremes.

Her eyes dilated into giant saucers, like an animal trapped by the terror of the moment. She whirled around, unsteady from dizziness and,

147

steadying herself with the corridor walls, made her way soundlessly to the door. Afraid of stumbling or drawing attention to herself she slipped out of the suite and then ran for all she was worth. Tears streamed down her face and her throat was seized with spasms.

She let out a silent scream – "Aaaaaah!" and then growled, like a mad, wounded and frenzied animal. As she bust out the back door of the building, she headed for the cement porch outside the storage room door and collapsed. Her sobs and wails kept on coming but she tried to stifle them by biting her fingers and covering her mouth.

"Mom...Mom...Mom!!!" It was unbearable. "Mom, you didn't like Nick from the start. You didn't even want me to date him! That's why! Now I understand. You were already his lover. You were cheating on me all along! And lying to me while you did it! You totally betrayed me! You were the only person I loved and trusted my whole life. I blindly believed you would never hurt me. Mom, how could you possibly do this to me? Why?"

Alana sobbed hysterically, scratching her fingernails on the cement. The intensity of her sobs soon led to convulsions, which overtook her and stole her breath. From despair her feelings struck out in hatred, first for Maria and once again, for Nick.

"You are an idiot!" she shouted, addressing him. "Why did I ever think you were wonderful? You are nothing but a fool – a blind fool. Who are you sleeping with? She is an old woman! An old witch! An old *bitch*! Are you crazy? Her body is sagging and wrinkled. Her vagina is flabby and her breasts sag! And you were kissing those droopy blobs of flesh! How could you make love to *her*? Why did I ever feel sorry for you? Well, Tracy was right, you are an idiot! And Jim was right, too, to laugh at you. You're not robbing the cradle; you're robbing the old folks' home! What a damn idiot you are. How could I ever fall for you in a million years?

"You are dirty! You are dirty pigs, both of you! Dirty pigs fucking! I hate you! I hate you both!"

Alana beat the cement with her balled fists until her hands were bruised. She even broke her diamond engagement ring in the process. The diamonds came off and scattered in the pre-dawn darkness. The ring itself was bent out of shape and hurt her finger. Angrily, she yanked it off and threw it as far as she could. The whole world appeared dark to her. Her consciousness was paralyzed by the emotional shock. She sank into a crumpled mass of sobs and self-pity and lost all sense of who or where she was.

Unaware of what was going on around her or of time passing, Alana was startled by the sound of a moving car. It scared and sobered her for a minute. She stopped her crying, crawled limply to the corner of the building and looked around it. She saw a taxi pull up in the back alley. The driver got out, walked to the back door and rang the service bell.

Alana didn't know how she knew it, but she realized that it was *their* taxi for the airport. She sat like a lump, mad and motionless, waiting for the couple to appear. The driver exited the building shortly, carrying suitcases and put them in his trunk. Behind him came Nick and Maria.

Maria was dressed elegantly in a red English suit and high heels – both Alana had never seen before. She looked so charming that it was even difficult to recognize her. Nick walked beside her, carrying his bag on his left shoulder. His right hand held Maria's waist.

Nick and Maria passed closely by where Alana was slumped around the corner. Her horror was reignited when she saw Nick's palm and fingers touch her mother's body. There was so much ownership in that touch. Unconsciously, he showed the whole world that this woman belonged to him forever. There was so much sincerity and deep love communicated that Alana couldn't believe her eyes. She had never seen Nick so happy, so confident, or so loving before.

Nick and Maria stopped beside the driver, and Nick gave him his bag to put into the trunk.

"Well, folks," the driver said. "Where're we headed?"

"To the airport," Alana heard Maria answer.

"To the Municipal or International Airport?"

"The International," replied Nick smiling broadly. "We're going to get married in Germany."

"Oh, congratulations, you two!" the driver said as he slammed the trunk shut.

Nick opened the backdoor for Maria and helped her get into the cab. Then he closed the door, and encircled the cab, as the driver opened the door for him.

The car window was down and Alana heard Nick asked Maria beside him, "By the way, little dolly, did you call Father Jorgen?"

"Yes," she answered, "he'll meet us at the airport."

Cabbie started his car and they pulled away from the building.

A wedding in Germany! In the blue Cathedral! With Father Jorgen! It was all too much! All of those were Alana's fondest dreams, based on Maria's stories. She craved to have it all one day for herself. And to have it with Nick. But now everything had been stolen away. Her love, her man, yes even the father of her unborn child had been stolen, along with cherished dream. It was more than she could possibly bear.

Alana covered her face with her hands and wept like a little girl. Her most precious dream had been plucked from her pocket by her own mother. Painfully, she now understood that the love that existed between Nick and Maria was not dirty or sordid; on the contrary, it was nearly divine – pure, deep and real. Everything was finished for Alana but, feeling so offended, she couldn't admit it.

"They took everything away and discarded me, like an old shoe…like an empty bag…like a used condom," she lamented her mind poisoned with hate. "I mean nothing to them, just some garbage."

They have each other and forgot about her. She'd never been more humiliated in her whole life. And to add to it all, they had plotted together against her.

Alana had heard Nick mention that Maria called him often during the last three days. When? Alana never heard her call anyone. Her mother must have done it when she was out. They were co-conspirators.

Nick had told her that he might be going to South America. It was all a lie! They were both trying to cheat on her. Her pain and despair led her deeper into crazed state. Something fundamental had snapped in her head, her heart and her soul.

"I hate you, hate you, *hate you!*" Alana cried out. "I'll get my revenge. I'll chase you down and hit you and kill you! You'll never have your wedding."

She stood up to run over to her car, but could only stagger and seize the storage room door handle to keep from falling. Unexpectedly the door gave way under the pressure of her body – might be that cleaners forgot to lock it – and Alana busted into the storage room, falling down, stumbling over something big and soft. It was the big garbage bag full of her stuffed animals that her mother had placed there. As Alana fell, the bag ripped and she reached deep inside feeling the plush fur of her collection.

"Oh it's you guys, damn it!" she shrieked. "You suck! It's all yours fault. You pushed him away from me! Oh, damn it to hell! I hate you, I hate you all!"

She tried to raise but suddenly felt a sharp pain in her stomach, and doubled over with a moaning growl. It was impossible to straighten up. Next, Alana saw that her uniform pants were wet from a hot fluid oozing from between her legs. She tried to muffle her anguish, now expressed in groans, as her teeth began chattering and she broke out in a cold sweat.

With horror, Alana realized that she was suffering a miscarriage. Now it would be impossible to drive and chase down the couple. She was suffocating with pain and unable to walk upright.

"Damn animals!" she shouted angrily, "I hate you! I'm gonna kill you!"

With that, Alana grabbed the broken bag and pulled it through the storage room, then through the hallway to her suite. She unlocked the door and pulled the bag into the kitchen. On her knees and shaking, she opened the cabinet drawer and grabbed the kitchen knife. With malice and revenge, she began stabbing at the plastic bag. Soon the stuffed animals fell out onto the linoleum and scattered. Sitting on the floor, Alana grabbed them one by one and methodically cut into each one with the blade and threw them across the room.

Before long, the kitchen was a mess of cotton, sawdust, down, plastic chips, sponge foam and plastic eyes in all colors. Teddy bears and fluffy dogs with ripped stomach, ears and legs were dismembered and stared at her with hollow eye sockets.

"I'll get even with you all," Alana spitefully promised them. "You made him dump me."

When they had all been destroyed, she felt extremely thirsty. Her body was dehydrated from losing so much blood, not to mention the tears and sweat. She really needed something to drink. Alana got up slowly and, without thinking, opened the refrigerator door. It was completely empty except for a lone champagne bottle. She and her mother had only had a little of it, and now there was just a half bottle left. That meant that Nick and Maria had shared some before they took the taxi. It was another arrow piercing her heart.

"They stole everything from me! They even stole my champagne!" she shouted unbelievably. "Even this! Everything!"

Still, with the kitchen knife in her hand, Alana grabbed the bottle from the fridge and drank it all. Her enormous gulps caused her to choke and cough. At least, the cold liquid served to cool her momentarily. But then the alcohol hit her bloodstream and inflamed her once more. She became more angry and hotter than ever.

Alana helplessly surveyed the room in her desperation to cause more havoc and exorcise the demons raging within her. She moved out of the kitchen and found something else to wreck. On the living room walls, where her mother's paintings once hung were faded rectangular outlines on the wallpaper.

In tears, Alana maneuvered herself into the empty living room and began to attack the walls with her knife. She slashed the drywall with all her might and left gashes for every perceived insult she had endured.

"I hate you, Mom!" she wailed. "I hate your fucking, stupid paintings! They are ugly! They broke my life!"

She was high now on champagne which temporary eased the pain in her stomach. Her drunken state empowered her to leap at the walls like a crazy woman. In fifteen minutes, it looked like five vandals had worked the apartment over: there were scratches, gouges, slits, and rips on all the surfaces. As the passion drained out of her, she surveyed the scene of destruction she had wrought with her tear-swollen face. Her toys were dead and mangled; the walls were scarred by a maniac. Alana was horrified by the evil clearly on display.

She had attacked the stuffed animals, the very symbols of her happy life with her mother. They represented her childhood and the precious gifts from her first love, Tom. That was her life before and now it had all been decimated.

"Why did you do this to me, Mom? I loved you. I trusted you. I believed in you, Mom," Alana moaned with regret and resentment. From all of her crying she had now lost her voice and squeezed the last tears from her eyes, which were red and completely fogged her vision. Her soul had burned like a flame and then had been smothered. Her gut was wrenched with insufferable emptiness and was as bottomless as the universe.

She was surrounded by a hellish atmosphere and there was no escape from it.

"Mom...Nick...Nick...Mom...!" Alana once more pictured them naked in bed together. She couldn't erase the image from her tortured mind. Sinking in despair with hatred, she felt she was trapped in this swamp forever and would never be able to wash all the contamination away. She was anxious to end this torment. If she could only stop breathing. Just find some place to sleep. To unconsciously slip into oblivion. To get away from all this, forever.

The piercing pain in her stomach grabbed her again.

With the knife still clutched in her hand, Alana waddled to the bathroom, growling and reeling against the corridor walls. She carefully placed the knife on the edge of the tub, then turned on the faucets and then frantically started tearing away her clothes. Her shoes, pants and panties were soaked with blood. It continued flowing down her streaked legs, reddened her feet and spilled onto the floor. Through her dizziness, she felt revulsion at the darkened stains that meant her child had died. With a valiant effort she flung her stripped body into the tub. Once there, she collapsed in the flowing water.

Quickly, the red water enveloped her form with warmth and tenderness. The pain in her belly gradually subsided and she entered a realm of calm, peace and rest. She turned the hot water on full and closed her weary eyes.

"I love you, Nick," she numbly mumbled. "Thank you...for teaching me...how to end... this torment...at last..."

At the airport in New York, Nick and Maria needed to change planes to Europe. They had a two hour layover between flights. They ate a late breakfast in the café, watched the planes take off and land for awhile and then retreated to seats in the departure lounge in front of the TV. There was nothing interesting on, just some commercials and the sound had been muted.

Nick sat relaxing, his arm around Maria's shoulder, sharing with her one of the moments from his new book.

"Are you listening to me?" he asked her suddenly, looking closely into her eyes.

"Yes, I am," she said a bit distractedly. "Sorry, my love. I'm just thinking…I'm so worried about Alana. She left me that urgent message on the phone but when I dialed her there was no answer."

"Maria, please," Nick interrupted her coldly. "Leave her alone. Let her grow up, finally. Oh, Jesus! Look at this!"

He stood suddenly and went over to the TV and turned up the sound. Maria shuddered. There was Gary Edwards on the screen. Nick returned to his seat, took Maria's hand and tensely squeezed it.

"Nick, you've got to control yourself," Maria whispered, sensing his agitation. She put her head on his shoulder and squeezed his hand in return.

"We are very proud, Mr. Edwards," the reporter was saying to Gary, "that the American Academy of Fine Arts, Fiction and Poetry has proposed your book *My Obsessive Passion* as a possible candidate for the Nobel Prize this year. We are really hoping that you'll get it. I'm sure the audience would like to know if you are writing your next book already."

Gary gave him an imprudent smile.

"You know," he slowly began in his usual manner. "I am really a one-hit writer. And, after all, what would be the purpose of writing a second book if nobody in human history ever got the Noble Price twice?"

"Oh," the reporter laughed. "That's true. It's a rule – nobody in human history got it twice. So, you are not writing anymore?"

Gary shrugged his shoulders.

"I have other plans."

"Oh, it must be something special," the reporter laughed again. "Would you like to share it with us, please?"

"Well, I'm waiting to become a proud father. My wife, Mrs. Laura Edwards, is expecting."

"Congratulations, sir!"

A young couple sitting behind Nick and Maria caught the show as well. At the moment as the reporter congratulated Gary, Nick overheard the young man asking his wife, "Can they be sure, honey that their child won't be born with a cat's face?" and they laughed together.

Nick and Maria exchanged glances and laughed too.

At the same morning hour, old Stan went downstairs to wash his dusty car. The parking lot was just about deserted and very quiet. Almost everyone had already gone to work. He went to his car and noticed that there was colored water dripping from a crack in the cement ceiling.

That's funny, he thought. Maybe there's a rusty leak somewhere. I better report it to Maria right away before any more damage is done. She should call the plumbers immediately and get it fixed.

Stan put his arthritic hand under the drops and was shocked to realize that it wasn't rust but blood that colored the liquid.

"Oh, my! This is serious!" he exclaimed and hobbled back to his suite to call the police.

At eight o'clock in the morning, the main entrance of the *River Valley* building was surrounded by two police cars and an ambulance truck. At that scheduled hour, a white van also pulled up. *The Georgia Show* was written with huge golden letters on its side. It was the film crew and the reporter who arrived to do the interview with Alana Miller. The cameramen, carrying the cameras on their shoulders proceeded to the caretaker's suite along with the paramedics and the police, who rushed the door…

When Nick and Maria, holding hands, entered through St. Peter's Cathedral gate, the deep blue light overwhelmed them. They felt bathed in its promise and miraculous atmosphere. It was like paradise, divine and uplifting! The large bell pealed somberly and slowly, enhancing the fantastic feeling. They couldn't help themselves: tears came to their eyes.

• • •

Three years later, the novel *Forgiveness* by Nicolas Bell (illustrated by Maria Bell) was nominated by the European Fiction Academy and won the Nobel Prize. The world press acknowledged that, judging by the level of the author's talent, this book could not be compared to anything ever, except to *My Obsessive Passion* by Gary Edwards, who had received the Nobel Prize three years earlier.

The similarity in style of the two books wasn't recognized by the media. Nobody in the world could ever guess that the real author of *My Obsessive Passion* was Nick Bell. His first book *My Wildfire Life* was stolen

154

and published as *My Obsessive Passion* under the name of the thief, Gary Edwards, who got the Nobel Prize. Nick had been the laureate in reality, but officially he wasn't.

However, now Nick got his own Nobel Prize for his second book, *Forgiveness*, published under his own name.

So, the genius who was awarded the Nobel Prize twice – did exist, but it was left a mystery buried in the historical list of the Nobel Prize Laureates.

In his interview with CNN Mr. Nicolas Bell remarked that his book, *Forgiveness*, was dedicated to the loving memory of his step-daughter Alana Miller, who had perished at a young age. The screen rights were bought for a forthcoming Hollywood production.

Nick also revealed that his next book, *Deadly Fate,* had just been completed and accepted by Random House. It told the story of the tragic immigration of German refugees over the Berlin Wall to new lives in America.

When quizzed about his future plans, Nick readily answered, "I'm starting to re-write an unpublished manuscript from my youth, *My Wildfire Life*. I expect it will be published before too long. Right now I have the germs of five more novels in my mind, so I'm sure you'll be hearing from me in the future."

In their third year of married life, Nicolas and Maria Bell adopted infant orphan twins. They named the pair Albert and Alana.

About the Author

KATE VALERY WAS BORN IN Moscow, Russia. She graduated from Moscow State Conservatory of Music as an expert in Western European Music History. For some time she worked at the Russian State Radio as a Music Editor in Programming and later – as a correspondent. Her first short story book *Moscow – The City and Its People* was published in 1985.

Later Kate Valery spent her full adventure years at four continents: Europe, Africa, Asia and America – and authored 10 more books in Russian and 3 in English. Now she is residing in Edmonton, Alberta.

About the Book

A SUDDEN CALL AT THE END OF the shift changed forever the life of a young, pretty security guard Alana Miller, and her mother's life, as well. They got involved accidentally in the frantic story of a talented writer who, thanks to them, survived his deadly collapse.

STOLEN is a subtle and deep psychological book, where European and American minds are clashing with each other and creating an unexpected outcome. In the rivalry between two women: daughter (22) and mother (62), a young millionaire chooses the oldest one.

STOLEN is an enthralling tale of deceit, betrayal and fantastically beautiful love – the love between the young man and the woman 27 years older than him. You wish it never ends; wish to find out more with the amazing characters depicted so colorfully by the author and you will be sad to part with them.